## Praise for *Upheaval: Stories*

"The first thing you notice about Chris H thenticity of voice and detail, opening windows into lives, opening out in unexpected directions, in a world scary as the morning news. They are stories of displacement, vulnerability, of longing for home in a time when the present is a foreign country. The stories of *Upheaval* thrill with the strangeness of the real, the intensity of human connections. They are narratives of upheavals that leave us with new insights and perspectives. In this age of wonderful storytellers, Chris Holbrook is one of our very best."—Robert Morgan, author of *Gap Creek: The Story of a Marriage*

"What Edith Wharton called 'the hard considerations of the poor' are at the troubled heart of these excellent stories. Holbrook's Appalachia is neither the sentimentalized Appalachia of Dollywood nor the demonized Appalachia of *Deliverance;* instead these stories do what the best regional literature has always done—find in one particular place what is true of all places. Despite his characters' economic status and Eastern Kentucky locale, they are true to all people in their humanity and complexity."—Ron Rash, author of *Serena: A Novel*

"Readers throughout the Appalachian region and beyond will be delighted by Holbrook's stories."—Tim Gautreaux, author of *The Missing: A Novel*

"Holbrook's perfect pitch for the dialect of the southern mountains delineates lonely, isolated people for whom ancestral traditions are dead, the future appears hopeless, and the desolate present, as their mountains are destroyed all around them, feels unbearable. This unique blend of bleak stoicism, sardonic humor, and menacing claustrophobia make this book a masterpiece for me—of both Appalachian fiction and of the short story form."—Lisa Alther, author of *Kinfolks: Falling Off the Family Tree*

## Praise for *Upheaval: Stories*, continued

"Ever since the release of Chris Holbrook's *Hell and Ohio,* many of us have been impatiently awaiting another collection by this master of the short story. *Upheaval* is well worth the fourteen-year wait. There is not one false note in this entire book, where Holbrook explores all the joys and faults and complexities of the place he knows and loves and understands so well. Each sentence is a tight and taut poem, each story an intimate, perfect epic. Holbrook is one of our best writers, and *Upheaval* immediately takes its place as one of *the* essential Appalachian books."—Silas House, author of *Clay's Quilt: A Novel*

# UPHEAVAL

# KENTUCKY VOICES

*Miss America Kissed Caleb*
Billy C. Clark

*The Total Light Process: New and Selected Poems*
James Baker Hall

*With a Hammer for My Heart: A Novel*
George Ella Lyon

*Famous People I Have Known*
Ed McClanahan

*Sue Mundy: A Novel of the Civil War*
Richard Taylor

*At The Breakers: A Novel*
Mary Ann Taylor-Hall

*Come and Go, Molly Snow: A Novel*
Mary Ann Taylor-Hall

*Nothing Like an Ocean: Stories*
Jim Tomlinson

*Buffalo Dance: The Journey of York*
Frank X Walker

*When Winter Come: The Ascension of York*
Frank X Walker

*The Cave*
Robert Penn Warren

# UPHEAVAL

*Stories*

Chris Holbrook

THE UNIVERSITY PRESS OF KENTUCKY

Several stories in this collection were previously published, some in slightly different form. "Somebody Known" appeared in *American Voice,* no. 47 (1998). "Christmas Down Home" appeared in *A Kentucky Christmas,* ed. George Ella Lyon (Lexington, Ky.: University Press of Kentucky, 2003). "New-Used" appeared in *Appalachian Heritage* 32, no. 1 (Winter 2004). "Upheaval" appeared in *Night Train,* no. III (2004) and in *Missing Mountains* (Nicholasville, Ky.: Wind Publications, 2005). The author would also like to thank the Kentucky Arts Council, whose support helped make this book possible.

The University Press of Kentucky

Scholarly publisher for the Commonwealth, serving Bellarmine University, Berea College, Centre College of Kentucky, Eastern Kentucky University, The Filson Historical Society, Georgetown College, Kentucky Historical Society, Kentucky State University, Morehead State University, Murray State University, Northern Kentucky University, Transylvania University, University of Kentucky, University of Louisville, and Western Kentucky University.


*Editorial and Sales Offices:* The University Press of Kentucky
663 South Limestone Street, Lexington, Kentucky 40508-4008
www.kentuckypress.com

13 12 11 10 09     5 4 3 2 1

Library of Congress Cataloging-in-Publication Data

Holbrook, Chris.
Upheaval : stories / Chris Holbrook.
p. cm. — (Kentucky voices)
ISBN 978-0-8131-9244-4 (pbk. : acid-free paper)
1. Kentucky—Fiction. I. Title.
PS3558.O347743U64 2009
813'.54—dc22

2009014234

This book is printed on acid-free recycled paper meeting the requirements of the American National Standard for Permanence in Paper for Printed Library Materials.

Manufactured in the United States of America.

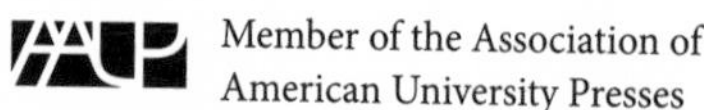

*To my wife, Mary Beth, and my daughter, Erin*

# CONTENTS

# SOMEBODY KNOWN

WHEN SOMEBODY WENT INTO Ruby Hall's house and tied her up and stole the shoe-box full of cash and savings bonds she'd kept hid behind a bag of quilt pieces in her closet and the cameo brooch she'd kept wrapped in an old duster in the middle drawer of her bureau and the silver-plated pocket watch of her late husband's she'd kept in a candy dish on her night table, everybody said it must have been somebody who knew her, knew she was an old widow woman living by herself that they could just go in on and have their way with.

The Sunday after, the sermon at the Right Fork Church of Christ was about finding refuge in God and strength in God and fearing not, though the waters roar and the mountains shake and fall to the sea. The city of God will not be moved. After the sermon, each of the church's twenty-three steady souls came forth to hug Ruby or touch her shoulder, to say "bless you" to her as if she'd suffered a death.

"This is like to happen again," Mabel Sturgill said. She was a tall, stout woman with gray, waist-length hair tied in a bun atop her head. She lingered in the churchyard with those who'd volunteered to help put Ruby's house back in order. "That girl of hers ought to get her tail back from Fort Wayne, Indiana," Mabel said, her face dark as she spoke, her black eyes narrow behind the high points of her cheekbones.

Doris Clarke grasped Mabel's forearm. "That girl's got three kids by three different men," she whispered.

The day was cold. Frost gleamed on the church house roof and on the timbers of the car bridge and the curled edges of fallen leaves. The westward slope of Auglin Mountain lay still in shade though its ridge was bright-lit, the sun glaring upon the bare knob of earth—of razed trees and gouged-up rock—in a harsh and judging way.

"Why, it's somebody that knowed her," Will Clarke said.

"Now, no," Bige Sturgill replied, his full, smooth face cringing with sudden worry, "I can't hardly believe that." He leaned against the side of his and Mabel's Oldsmobile, shaving the hair from the back of his wrist with Will Clarke's Case knife while Will snapped the blades open and shut on Bige's Sodbuster.

"It's a wonder," Doris Clarke began, then stopped to motion Mabel and a few of the other women closer so that the men might not hear. After she'd spoken, they all nodded to each other with pained expressions.

The sound of a coal truck stilled further talk. They stood watching the little twist of road that ran by the church as the truck whipped around the curve, diesel smoke belching black into the air, gravel and clods of mud and black water spraying from the wheels, chips of coal and slate flying from the jarring, rattling bed. The driver blared his horn in passing and broke to pieces whatever calm and lightness the morning might still have held.

They found Ruby Hall's house less plundered than expected. In the kitchen, a container of sugar had been knocked from a counter, and a few cabinet doors hung open. In the middle of the spilled sugar, chunks of dried mud outlined the lugged sole of a work boot. Storage boxes and bags had been spilled from the bedroom closet, though Ruby's dresses hung undisturbed next to her late husband's shirts. The sheets had been stripped from the bed and the mattress and box springs upended. The bureau drawers had all been emptied. Ruby's underclothes lay in piles amidst still-folded towels and sheets and the squares of bright-colored cloth she used for quilting.

Ruby sat on the couch in the living room, a tiny woman with

thin gray hair and thin pale skin hued with bluish veins. She clutched both hands to her chest, her fingers knotted together. From time to time she freed a trembly hand to wipe her eyes, and Mabel paused each time to pat her shoulder.

"Tell me what all they touched, honey," Mabel said.

"I'm ashamed for you to see my house like this," Ruby replied. She shifted her eyes and blinked whenever Mabel or Doris or anyone looked at her directly.

Mabel's face burned while she worked. When the other women let up in their cleaning, she'd say, "Let's do this one more thing," and the women would look at each other long enough to sigh, then hurry to their new chores. They swept and mopped the kitchen floor and cleaned the counter and washed a week's worth of dirty dishes. They laundered, folded, and put away the clothes and sheets and towels that had been dumped on the bedroom floor. They took down, washed, and rehung the curtains.

Ruby's spirits rose as the house became cleaner. Late in the day, when the women took a break for coffee and a bite of the apple cake Doris had brought, Ruby spoke of her daughter and grandchildren. "She's got the prettiest babies," she said, showing around a framed 8 × 10 of the three children, all girls, with their mother.

Mabel sat next to Ruby on the couch and studied the picture. The girls and their mother all had blond hair, though the mother's was unnaturally light. They all smiled the same way, their teeth gritted, a false, forced smile for the camera that made even the two-year-old look devilish and mean.

"They're just as sweet as candy," Ruby said, touching her fingers to the children's glossy images. For the first time, Mabel noticed the reddish, ropelike scrape on the woman's forearm.

By evening the house was as clean as they could make it. Instead of dust and mildew, it smelled of Doris's apple spice cake. "Now you-all go on," Ruby said, "and don't worry about me. You've done enough." Her hands had become trembly again, and she clasped them together as if they were cold.

Each of the women hugged Ruby in leaving and said, "Lord love you," and Ruby said, "Lord love you" to them. Mabel paused in the doorway after the others had gone out, as if thinking of something else to do.

"I believe I'll piece you a quilt," Ruby whispered, as she and Mabel clasped hands. At first Mabel thought to warm Ruby's fingers, though the longer she held the poor woman's hands, the colder she felt herself become. Ruby clung tightly, her grip almost painful in its strength. She gazed into Mabel's face, her eyes wide and childlike and a little senseless. Mabel felt a sudden shiver of fear before Ruby's grip went weak.

"Now if you hear the slightest noise," Mabel said, "you call you somebody. You call the police or you call Bige and me."

Ruby closed her door and clicked the new lock Bige had installed.

"I don't know if I'll be able to sleep this night," Mabel said to herself, and she didn't. She dreamed all night of rogues and thieves. Twice she woke Bige to go look about some noise she thought she had heard. At four in the morning, she got out of bed, turned on all the lights in the house, and made a pot of coffee.

"I feel weak all over," she said to Bige when he came into the kitchen at six thirty.

"Will Clarke said it was somebody that knowed her," Bige said. "I can't hardly believe that." He poured a cup of coffee, took a sip, and frowned. "This coffee's thick as mud," he said.

"It used to be nobody even thought about locking their doors at night," Mabel said. "Not in this country. That girl of hers. Ooohh, I'd like to choke her."

"Our own kids have moved off," Bige said. He pulled a chair from the kitchen table and sat.

"It's not the same," Mabel said. "Steven and Bonnie call almost every day to check on us. And you know they'd be here in a heartbeat if anything bad happened."

"They don't call every day," Bige said.

"It's got to where all that's left hereabouts is old people," Mabel said. "Old people and the rogues that thieve off of 'em. I wish . . ." She hushed then and slumped back in her chair, crossing her arms and staring hard at the frosty kitchen window that was just brightening with daylight.

"Mabel," Bige said, "would you make me a fresh pot of coffee?"

At eight o'clock Mabel still sat, tired and trembly, at the kitchen table. She had been listening for several minutes to a tapping-scratching sound at the kitchen door, a sound like the wind would make or like some small, sly animal, scrapping about for food. When she cracked open the door, she saw shaggy hair and beard and smoldering cigarette. "Bige," she called, hurrying to the living room, "there's somebody at the kitchen door. Trying to get in."

Bige put down the western novel he was reading, looked into Mabel's face for a moment, and pushed himself from his recliner. His knee popped as he rose, and if Mabel hadn't put out a hand to steady him, he would have plopped back into the chair again.

"Wait," she called. "Wait." But Bige was already hobbling toward the kitchen, his loose shoestrings flapping about his feet as he fished in his shirt pocket for his upper plate. Mabel followed quickly after, urging him to be careful.

The young man hovered on the threshold, hunched inside a quilted overshirt that was coming undone at the shoulder seams and high-backed overalls so thin and frazzled that the gallus hooks and rivets were wearing loose from the denim. For a few moments after Bige opened the door, none of them spoke. Then the young man rolled his shoulders as if to warm himself. "You-all need any roofing work done?" he asked. He stared hard at his feet after he'd spoken.

"Who are you?" Bige asked.

"My daddy's John Sloane," the man said. "I'm Luther." He looked up just barely enough to meet their eyes.

"We don't need no kind of work done," Mabel said.

"John Sloane from over on Big Branch that married a Sizemore?" Bige asked.

"Mommy's name is Agnes," Luther said, smiling crookedly

through his beard. "They've been moved to Cincinnati twelve years now."

"I know your people," Bige said. He took Luther's elbow to pull him into the house, but Luther held back until he could slip off his brogans and set them outside the door. He stepped inside, barely farther than the threshold, in dirty white socks, the smell of cigarettes strong about him.

"We don't need no work done," Mabel said.

"It's John Sloane's boy," Bige said. "Luther. John and Agnes Sloane. Their boy."

Mabel stared hard at Bige. She frowned and shook her head no at him, but he was looking at Luther Sloane and grinning. She tugged at his shirtsleeve. "Bige," she said. "Bige." Finally she threw up her hands and turned her back to her foolish husband. "Tell him to come in or stay out," she said. "Do one or the other."

For a long while she paced the floors, on the edge of flying to the closet for Bige's .410 shotgun. She crept a few times down the hallway to within earshot of the kitchen, but it was mostly Bige she heard, his voice raised loud for the sake of his own dull hearing. He told about the worn-out kitchen tile, about the sags in the floor, about the cracked plaster in the bedroom walls, and on and on. He told about the arthritis in both his knees and the blood clot he'd had in the calf of his right leg. He even told about the partial blockage she had in the big artery that ran up the side of her neck and about how she was not to drip bacon grease on her bed lettuce anymore or she might cause herself a stroke someday. He sat right there in that kitchen and told how Steven and Bonnie lived far off and didn't come to visit but very seldom, told that to beardy, ragged-looking Luther Sloane for no good reason but that he claimed kin with John and Agnes Sloane that once upon a time had lived on Big Branch, when as far as that went this Luther might not even be John and Agnes's boy.

After a while she willed herself to cease her pacing and sit. She opened her Bible into her lap and rocked, too on edge still to read the words of scripture but calmed by the sight of graceful letters, by the touch of worn pages and cracked binding, by the simple weight of the book. For a while she studied the Bible's frontispiece, the figured image of God the creator—grim and bearded as a mountain pastor—in golden, holy light above the formless waste; and on the page after, the generations-old record of her own family's names and birth dates.

The oldest entry was for her great-great-grandmother—rough, mean old Granny Sal—equal mix of Cherokee and Black Irish. Mabel's mother had used to tell her she was Granny Sal made over. It wasn't just eye and hair color she meant, Mabel knew. It was temper. Well, I'll show some temper, she thought, that Sloane so much as looks cross-eyed at me. The newest entry was for Steven's littlest girl, Ladonna. They had last visited at Easter. Ladonna had worn a yellow dress and black patent leather shoes with little buckles and white socks and a white straw bonnet banded with a yellow ribbon. She'd clung to her daddy's legs and hardly spoken, and Mabel had had to coax her with an Easter basket full of M&M's and marshmallow eggs and stuffed toy animals just to get a hug.

"It's not true," Mabel said to Bige when he came into the living room sometime later.

"What's not true?" Bige asked. He settled heavily into his recliner and took up his western novel once more.

"What you said about Steven and Bonnie never coming to visit."

"I said no such a thing," Bige said.

"Well, it's not true."

Bige flipped through the pages of his novel for a while, as if unsure of where he'd left off. Then he put down the book and laced his fingers across his stomach. "I've hired that Sloane boy to take up our old kitchen tile and put down new," he said, "and to patch the soft spots in the floor."

Mabel closed her Bible, pressing her palms flat against the cover. "You watch him," she said, without looking up. "Bige, you watch that jasper."

The first day, Luther and Bige heaved aside her refrigerator and stove and washer and dryer so that Luther could pry off the toe molding from around the walls and pull up the tile and get at whatever flooring had rotted. She listened all day to the shriek of nails being pulled, of floorboards being ripped from joists. By that evening, her kitchen was a shambles of displaced appliances and scraps of old tile and flooring and rusty nails. A third of the floor had been taken up, leaving a hole covered by just a sheet of clear plastic.

Mabel ended the day with a headache so bad she couldn't close her eyes for seeing swirls of black dots. Every time she tried to rest, she got so dizzy she'd have to open her eyes again and sit up and focus on some still object.

When Steven called, she barely felt strong enough to hold the phone to her ear. "I've been up two nights straight with Ladonna," he said, his voice hoarse and low-toned. "She's had a bad earache."

"Why ain't you took her to the doctor?" Mabel asked.

"He said not to bring her in unless her temperature went above 103," he said. "We've been giving her doses of children's Tylenol and penicillin and keeping her temperature down with wet cloths."

"I'd a took her in," Mabel said. "I'd a took her in no matter what anybody said."

"We're doing what we need to," Steven said. Then he said something she couldn't make out, something muffled-sounding, as if he'd put his hand over the receiver so he could speak to someone else without her hearing.

"You keep that child's head covered when you take her outside," Mabel said. "You keep socks on her feet even when she's in the house."

"It was a virus she got at daycare," Steven said.

"That old daycare," Mabel said. "She ought not to have strangers tending to her."

"How's Dad?" Steven asked, his voice suddenly sharp and so loud that Mabel paused and pressed her fingers to her temples before answering.

"Don't you worry about Dad," she said. "There's not a thing wrong with Dad. Listen—"

"How's your blood pressure?" Steven asked.

"Listen," Mabel said. "Listen."

"Have you heard from Bonnie?"

"I've got a good thermal blanket I'm going to send up," Mabel said. "Listen to me."

"That's all right," Steven said.

"Steven!" Mabel shouted into the phone. "Listen, somebody broke into Ruby Hall's house. Came in on her in broad daylight. Tied her up and pilfered everything she had. Her all alone. Not a soul to look after her."

"Ruby Hall?" Steven asked.

"You *know* you know Ruby Hall," Mabel said. "That goes to our church. Listen, Bige has hired this boy to work on our kitchen. He's a awful-looking feller."

"Ladonna's all right," Steven said. "She's fine. I'll call next weekend and you can talk to her."

"Listen," Mabel said. "Steven." For a moment after Steven hung up, Mabel's head felt clear. Then suddenly she became so dizzy again she could not rise from her rocker or even move. She sat holding the receiver, the hum of the dial tone loud throughout the room, until she heard Bige's heavy, clunking steps upon the front porch. She rose then, her arms and legs trembling in a way that made her a little afraid.

The next day Bige headed into town to pick up the new kitchen tile. Sit on the courthouse steps and swap knives, Mabel thought. "Go on," she told him as he left, "I'll try not to get knocked in the head while you're away."

All morning Mabel sat with her rocker facing the kitchen while Luther worked. Once she caught herself dozing, lulled by the sound of Luther's handsaw. At noon she gave him a dinner of cold bologna sandwiches and warm pop. She sat at the kitchen table with him, her chair jammed against the refrigerator, and watched him suffer through his meal.

Luther never spoke while he ate, though he would glance at

Mabel from time to time, and sometimes he would grin at her. *I'm watching you, buddy*, she wanted to say. *You better know it*.

That evening she said to Bige, "I don't trust that Luther."

"He's a good hand to work," Bige said. "He takes after his daddy that way."

"I don't trust him no further than I can throw him," Mabel replied. "And you ought not to either."

By nighttime Mabel's headache had eased enough for her to fall asleep, though she woke barely an hour later, unsure at first that she was even in her own house. She lay awake, thinking about Ladonna's earache and about Ruby Hall living out her days alone and uncared for. She thought about Bonnie chasing hither and yon after the army man she'd married, living the world over.

She thought about the day, years ago, when her little Bonnie had been lost. She had been canning kraut in Liz Holliefield's kitchen, chopping up cabbage heads while Bonnie played on the floor. For some reason, Mabel had left the kitchen, and when she'd come back Bonnie was gone from among the empty Mason jars and lids and rings where she'd been playing.

They had searched the house from cellar to eaves and then the yard and then the hillside. They had walked the length of the holler calling Bonnie's name. At every house neighbors had turned out to join the search. Mabel had finally sent Steven to bring Bige from his job. Bige had come still wearing his miner's cap, his hands and face still grimed with coal dust. They had looked into Truman Hayes's well then, and Bige and Steven had climbed to the old drift mine on the ridge top above Liz Holliefield's. They had found her just after dark, curled up asleep in the manger of Bennet Conley's barn, a canning ring dangling like a bracelet from her wrist.

That barn was gone now. The neighbors who'd helped search were gone—Truman Hayes, who'd had trailing at his heels always a mangy, redbone hound as old and crippled as its master; and Shirley Bledsoe, who'd been widowed young, who'd been a seamstress and quilt maker and made a good enough living by that trade to raise three children and not remarry; and Dave Mobley, who'd owned a tall, yellow mule; and poor old Liz Holliefield, who'd had a goiter on her neck the size of a mushmelon. They had all passed on. Their houses stood empty.

Mabel slept a few hours the next morning while Luther finished rebuilding the kitchen floor, slept through all the hammering and clatter of lumber that somehow was more easeful to her now than the middle of the night quiet. She woke just before noon with a sour taste in her mouth, like cabbage and white vinegar.

At dinner, Bige showed Luther the three-bladed Old Henry with the staghorn handle he'd taken in trade for his Sodbuster, and Luther showed Bige his plastic-handled Schrader with the locking blade. They talked a long while about knife brands and what sort of steel was easiest to hone and what kept an edge better and how to keep tarnish off.

When he finished eating, Luther sat quietly for a while, staring at the little crust of light bread left on his plate. At first Mabel thought he wanted something more to eat. He looked up then, past Bige's shoulder to where Mabel stood against the refrigerator. "It's getting to be where I get by on odd jobbing," he said. "Carpentry and plumbing and house painting. Cathy don't much like where we live. It's so far off the main roads. She'd rather be in Cincinnati or some such place. I believe my boy fares better here. I've not had to go on the welfare. I can't see it as long as I'm able to work. Can you?"

For a while Mabel didn't answer, surprised at first that he had spoken to her. "No," she finally said. "If a body can work, he ought to."

Luther smiled. Then he rose from the table and went outdoors to smoke a cigarette.

That afternoon Mabel tried to call Bonnie at the army base she lived on in Georgia. She tried to call Steven up in Michigan. She tried to call Ruby Hall. Late in the day her worry turned to dizziness and headache again, to rigid pain from neck to temples that she subdued barely by the pressure of her fingers.

Just before dark she had Bige drive her to Ruby Hall's house. They knocked on the door for a long while before Bige tried the knob and found it unlocked. "Oh, Lord," Mabel said as the door swung open. "Oh, Lord, Bige."

The house was dim, the curtains drawn. There was no sign of movement, no sound but the too-loud voice of a TV preacher. Mabel and Bige crept quietly across the threshold, both holding their breaths against the faint, frightening odor of something rancid that lingered beneath the scent of dust in the stale air.

Ruby lay upon the couch in the darkened living room, the TV light flickering upon her still face. Her skin looked blanched, her features contorted.

Mabel raised one hand to shield her eyes from the sight of Ruby's motionless figure. She looked instead at the TV, focused on the televangelist stalking boldly across his wide stage, shouting his singsong mix of scripture and nonsense words, slapping the flat of his palm hard against the foreheads of the poor afflicted, one after another, who fell then, their bodies rigid with healing power, into the arms of dark-suited attendants.

Mabel made a small cry, so odd a sound for her that Bige reached to steady her with his own slightly trembling hands. Ruby stirred then. Her eyes flickered from the depths of her deathlike sleep. She was still yet drawing breath.

"We thought you was murdered," Bige said and shut off the blaring TV.

"What?" Ruby mumbled. "Who?" She tried to raise herself on the couch, her arms waving, her hands groping like a drowning person's.

Mabel herself sank to the waiting perch of a ladder-back chair. She stared at Ruby as Bige helped the old woman sit up.

"Are you faring all right?" Bige shouted.

"I reckon I am," Ruby answered. "How are you?"

"You might as well invite the robbers in!" Mabel snapped.

"What, honey?" Ruby asked.

Mabel rocked herself in the straight-legged chair and glanced at Ruby.

"You left your door unlocked," Bige said gently.

"I did?" Ruby asked.

"Anybody so foolish," Mabel blurted. "Anybody that'd lay about with the door wide open. Don't you even remember getting robbed? Don't you even care for your own welfare? Ought to get knocked in the head. Ought to get sent to Danville, sent to the asylum and shut up in a room."

"I thought I locked that door," Ruby quavered. "I swear I don't remember."

"A person's got to look out for theirselves," Mabel said. "A person's got to look out for their own well being and not trust it all to somebody else. Let alone somebody not even no kin to you." Mabel hushed then. She rocked angrily in the stiff chair, her arms crossed on her chest. For a while she stared at the quilting frames set up in the corner, at the squares of cloth, the roll of cotton backing.

Ruby sat quietly, shifting her startled, owlish eyes from Mabel to Bige.

Before they left, Mabel straightened the kitchen a little and made sure Ruby had food enough. She had Bige take out the garbage that had begun to reek throughout the house.

"A person's not safe in their own home with the doors locked," Mabel said when they were in the car. "I'd as soon be dead and in the ground than in such a state as that Ruby's in. Not mind enough to care for herself. Not nobody to rely on."

"I don't believe you mean that," Bige said.

"Believe it," Mabel replied.

"You can't be untrusting of everybody," Bige said. "You can't all the time dwell on what might happen. That ain't no way to live."

The next day, Luther came to work carrying a tarnished bread pan covered by a sheet of aluminum foil. When Mabel opened the door, he reached it to her with both hands. His face was rosy with cold, his cheeks plumped by the little bit of smile he had. For a second Mabel wondered what he would look like clean-shaved. When she didn't take the pan right away, he pulled it back, and his face became stiff and lean once more. "It's not the first Cathy's made," he said. "It's not real bad." He reached the pan to her again, and this time she accepted.

She pulled a corner of the foil back and breathed the pungent scent of sage and pork meat and red pepper. "I can't eat souse," Mabel said. "It's too much salt for my blood pressure."

"I can eat it well enough," Bige said. He took the pan from Mabel, peeled back the foil, and pinched off a bite of the loaf with his fingers. "Man, that's good," he said. "The hotter the better, that's how I like it."

That day Luther rolled out the new linoleum. He crawled across it on his hands and knees, his boots off so he wouldn't scuff or muddy the clean, new surface. Mabel watched as he measured and cut, squaring the linoleum into the corners, piecing seams so they wouldn't show—his tape measure whirring on its spool, his pocket-knife slicing straight along pencil lines with hardly a pause. Bige was right, Mabel finally decided; Luther was a good hand to work.

Before the day was through, Mabel snuck around the house to the kitchen door where Luther had left his brogans. She picked up each boot on the end of a long stick and studied the soles for a long while. That evening Mabel felt a pinprick tingling in the fingers of her right hand that slowly turned to numbness as far as her elbow. She sat in her rocker and read her Bible until the feeling in her arm returned and her mind was enough at ease for her to go to bed.

She woke at midnight to the sough of wind, to the tick of roof beams and floorboards pinching tight with cold. She lay abed, unable to shut her eyes for seeing Ruby Hall sewing her quilts to the light of a televised ministry while beardy Luther Sloane, in threadbare overalls and muddy brogans, snuck upon her in the dark, grinning his sneaking grin.

Not mind enough to live, she whispered to herself, then rose to pace the house. Through the hallways hung with Steven and Bonnie's photographs. Through their bedrooms—Steven's piles of comic books and shelves full of model cars; Bonnie's Barbie dolls, her little porcelain figurines of horses. Through the paneled family room—Bige's recliner; her rocker; the oak coffee table, its surface dented by Bige's forever dropping of pocketknives and coins and keys; her mother's mantel clock that still ticked and kept time but had not chimed since Steven, when he was seven, pried it apart with a screwdriver. Through the kitchen—her old cabinet with the built-in flour bin and sifter that had come by truck in 1960 from Kingsport, Tennessee; her stove and sink and shelves. Each familiar room she passed through, each familiar thing she touched, seemed strange now, made so by the nighttime and silence and by her own sleeplessness.

She sat before the telephone in the early morning hours, threatening to call Steven up in Michigan or Bonnie down in Georgia and tell them what she thought of thankless children who forgot where they came from and grandkids who barely knew their own people.

The next morning as she drank her first cup of coffee, Mabel felt a sudden weakness, a sudden spilling out of strength from her arms and legs that made her tremble. She watched her hands begin to shimmer and then blur around her coffee cup, and she felt herself lean in her chair.

When her senses returned, she was lying on the new tile floor, her hand in a puddle of cold coffee next to the broken mug. Where's Bige? she thought. She tried to speak his name, but her face and tongue were numb and she could not make the sounds right. She tried to push herself up then but didn't feel strength enough to even move.

Bige is still asleep, she thought. In a minute here he'll wake up and come find me. From where she lay, she could see the puckers in the new tile where it had begun already to rise from the floor. She could see little patches of grime underneath the cabinets and fingerprints on the toe molding along the wall. She could hear the kitchen clock ticking, though she could not see its face. She could hear the refrigerator humming and feel its vibrations through the floor, and every so often she heard the water pump in the basement kick on. She began to count time by that sound.

Could Bige be up and gone already? she thought after a while. Could he be up and gone and me not know it? Could he have gone out and not seen me laying here?

She heard the footsteps then, coming from outside the house. Too light and quick to be Bige's, they circled the house two or three times—crunching as if on snow or frozen ground—then stopped by the kitchen door. She heard a few soft knocks. Then she heard Bige's name being called and then her own. It was Luther Sloane.

At first Mabel thought to call out. She could make sound enough to be heard still. But then she saw in her mind's eyes the muddy boot track in Ruby Hall's kitchen. She saw Luther's muddy brogans, his shaggy hair and beard and sneaky smile. She saw his Schrader-brand pocketknife with the locking blade.

She lay still and listened to him call their names again. Bige's and then hers. She listened to him knock and knock. She heard the door knob begin to rattle. She closed her eyes and began to pray for the Lord's deliverance.

# CHRISTMAS DOWN HOME

IT WAS THE MIDDLE of the day before they crossed into Kentucky. Wayne was less tense now, though he'd been so agitated in the morning that Kharmin had made him go wait in the car until she could get herself and Ashton packed and out the door. For the first hour of the trip he'd grieved over how much time they were losing by not beating the morning traffic out of town. He'd complained about how congested a town Dayton was and how dirty it looked with the streets covered in frozen sludge and the plowed snow drifts polluted with exhaust fumes and with stack smoke from the Frigidaire and General Motors plants. "Black snow," he'd said. "I don't see how anybody can enjoy Christmastime having to endure black snow."

It was the kind of comment he'd been making since Thanksgiving—about how dirty the streets were, about how rude the people were. You couldn't tell it was Christmas. Not Christmas like it should be, not Christmas like it was down home. Kharmin had not said outright how tired she was of him complaining, had not spoken in any regards directly to the issue of his carping remarks. Still yet, Wayne knew the words they'd had that morning had nothing to do with how late a start they were making, or with Ashton's behavior, or with anybody's hurt feelings, really.

He thought she ought to know, though, that it was just the stress of the season working on him, him dreading the long drive, dreading the weather. Right up until they left he'd kept glued to the Weather Channel, following the path of a high-pressure system building into Georgia and Tennessee, trying to time its convergence with the Arctic front descending from Canada. He ought not to have to tell her.

They'd had just one blowup thus far on the trip, when Ashton had made her request to stay over a day in Lexington so they could go see the light display at the Kentucky Horse Park. Wayne had tried explaining to his daughter in as patient a way as he could about not wanting to risk the weather.

When he'd peeked in the rearview mirror, he'd seen her sitting with her arms crossed, her hair raked forward to cover her face so completely that not even the tip of her nose showed, acting like she'd not even heard him. And then she'd started in her whining. She'd *always* wanted to see the Christmas lights at the Kentucky Horse Park. She'd never get another chance, probably. Why couldn't they just once do something she wanted to do.

Then Kharmin had chimed in. "Why couldn't we?"

And that had tore it. "No," he'd said, and crossed his hands before him in a gesture of making his word final. "We need to keep moving. The weather report's got rain almost to Jackson."

It irked him, them two allied together in such a way as to oppose him. Don't you know what a hazard it is driving in this weather? he'd wanted to say. Don't you get it?

When he'd turned to Kharmin for some sign of understanding, what he'd got was that look of hers with her eyebrows arched up above her glasses and her chin pressed to her chest and her lips pinched together so hard they lost their color. It flat burned him up, her looking at him like that, like it was him the one being unreasonable, being childish. Don't give me no stern warnings, he'd thought to say; I'm not one of your pupils. But he was no more liable to face down that look than her littlest sixth grader would've been.

It made matters no better when the thought came to him, What would it hurt to stay over a day in Lexington? Stay over and wait out the weather a day. He'd tried to think what to say then, but he could contrive no way to reverse himself. "You know what'll happen if that rain starts to freeze," he'd said.

They drove a long while without anybody speaking again, through that rolling north-central Kentucky pastureland that still yet held too much of a resemblance to southern Ohio for Wayne's satisfaction. It wasn't until they'd left behind the last exit to Lexington and were coming near to Stanton that Wayne ventured to break the silence.

"I hope we do get a little snow up home," he said.

Kharmin was bunched up against her door with her eyes closed, though, and Ashton was so self-diverted, twining and untwining the tips of her hair, that he got no more response than if he'd not even spoken.

"Well, what do you think, Wayne?" he asked himself aloud. "Wouldn't it be nice to have some snow up home for Christmas?"

He looked in the rearview mirror again. Ashton had lowered her head a little more. Wayne could see her eyes, just barely, beneath the long strands of hair hanging across her face. She looked like the victim of a punishing wind.

"I think it would be nice," he said to himself in reply. "Yes sir, some snow would be awful pretty." And then. "There's nothing like it when it snows up home. The way it covers the ridges. The way it lays on the trees. Lays on the creek where it's froze." He began to lift his hands from the steering wheel as he spoke, drawing the picture before him. "Everything so much more clean looking. So much more peaceful. Icicles hanging from the roofs of people's houses. Little bit of wood smoke in the air. The way the sun hits the frost of a morning, makes it dazzle." He tried telling them about sledding: "We'd break down a big cardboard box and use it to skid off the slope of the pasture." He asked if anybody had ever eaten snow cream, "where you take snow and mix it in with sugar and whole cream and eat it while it's still froze?" He was on the point of giving up when Ashton finally broke.

"All right!" she yelled.

Wayne hushed, satisfied just to have provoked a response. There was some silence still to be endured, he knew. But the mad spell would soon be over. In a minute they'd be talking amongst themselves, talking about school probably, gossiping about relatives probably. There'd be griping and complaining still yet, he knew. It made no difference though. And it made no difference that he would hardly be included in their talk. What mattered was them all getting along better, getting along better the way they ought to at Christmastime. He could even imagine Kharmin reaching over to give his hand a squeeze by way of saying "way to go," "Merry Christmas," "I love you," something like that.

When he glanced over at Kharmin he thought he caught her about to smile. It came to him the way he'd been talking. He'd got the accent back in his voice, the way of talking he'd begin to fall into whenever he crossed the Ohio River going south, but that he lost the gist of again when he came back north.

It came to him what she might be thinking about to almost smile. It came to him she might be thinking about the first time she'd heard him twang, about their first trip to meet his family. What she'd thought back then (what she'd said she'd thought) was that he was making fun, making a joke on the place he'd come from. "I'm marrying a hillbilly," she'd said. He'd laughed with her, though for the rest of the trip he'd acted so nervous he'd hardly spoken, and when he did he was so careful to speak properly, to sound out his *-ing*'s and correct himself whenever he said *ain't* instead of *aren't* that it had been almost painful to listen to himself. It came to him that maybe that was what she was thinking about now, and he laughed now to share the mood of recollection with her. She didn't laugh back though.

As they left the Mountain Parkway at Campton, Wayne was feeling better enough almost to forget his dread of the weather conditions. The countryside had begun to rise. Soon the coming horizon would rise up, becoming hills and mountains finally. It was just two more counties to cross. Just an hour and a half more of driving—two if they took it slow, if they kept cautious.

In a little while they'd come rolling up to the house, come tromping in with their Christmas packages and bowls of food. There'd be his daddy sitting by the fireplace, cracking black walnuts on the hearthstone. There'd be his mommy in the kitchen, thawing out the turkey, paring apples to make stack cake. The TV would be on to some old Christmas movie or to a bowl game maybe. It might be one or two of his brothers would be there, or one of his sisters might be in. Everybody with their kids. It wasn't Christmas without a house full of kids.

The first trace of weather came just before Jackson, a fine mix of sleet and rain so slight it seemed barely to wet the road surface. At first Wayne thought to drive faster to keep ahead of the cold front. After another mile or so though, the first few flakes of real snow began to fall. In the distance could be seen the heavy dark clouds. The oncoming cars all had their lights on, their wipers going.

Wayne made no mention of his returning dread. The pleasant talk he'd hoped for seemed doubtful still. What talk there was, was effort-making still. It was Kharmin asking a question of Ashton, Ashton then coming back with smart remarks or half answers, but not at least with silence. The stubbornness at least had give out. The sulkiness at least had give out. It had come to be almost peaceful-seeming in the car, almost cheerful-seeming. If not for the threat of worsening roads, Wayne might've settled in for an easeful drive.

There were patches of snow along the road shoulder now, and it had begun to stick to the roadway along the centerline. The blacktop shone with moisture. A fine white mist flowed slantwise across the headlight beams. It occurred to Wayne that he might ought to stop in Hazard and pick up a can or two of cashews. It wouldn't be Christmas without cashews, without cashews and a box of chocolate-covered cherries.

A small pickup truck came sailing around in the passing lane, its rear end fishtailing slightly. Wayne tensed and fought the urge to lay on his brakes. Further ahead the traffic had begun to slow, and when he looked in the rearview mirror Wayne could see a line of vehicles accumulating for half a mile behind.

He wished for a hot cup of coffee, a hot cup of coffee and a bite of something to ease his nerves. He thought about the spiral-cut ham they were bringing. It had come to be a tradition, them bringing in a spiral-cut ham. He thought about it sitting in the center of his mother's big table, the foil pulled back just enough to let a little steam rise. He imagined everybody praising the aroma, praising the tenderness of the meat that could be cut with a butter knife.

He thought too about the jam cake Aunt Reva would've sent down already, about the pan of peanut-butter fudge Aunt Daria would've sent up. It'd be the first thing he did when they got home, get a cup of coffee and a slice of that jam cake he looked forward to all year.

Suddenly he became aware of Ashton's voice right in his ear. He caught himself before telling her to quiet down. She said something again, more loudly still, and he realized then it was him she was speaking to. "What?" he asked.

"I said, 'We should've stopped in Lexington,'" she replied, then pointed through the windshield to indicate the snowfall.

Wayne kept himself from saying anything in response. It was an uproar she wanted, no doubt. He had asked his mamaw once who in the family she thought Ashton most favored. The old woman had thought about it a long while, named three or four people—her own sister, Rilla, who was so contrary she could barely stand anybody's company but her own, and that middle girl of Rilla's, that Suzie, who'd been so meek and fretful as a child she'd hardly ever spoken. Then too in some ways she thought Ashton favored Wayne's Aunt Reva, though she couldn't say how exactly. Aunt Reva was known for her kindliness. It was her the one always taking care of everybody, always catering to whoever was sick, always making the peace whenever a dispute arose. When Wayne and Kharmin were first married, Aunt Reva had sent them a ten-dollar bill in the mail every week for six months.

As much as Wayne would've liked to have seen some few of Aunt Reva's traits borne out in Ashton, to his mind, at least, they'd none come to fore. Finally his mamaw had just thrown up her hands and said, "She's a puzzle." Still yet, it might be something to it that she maintained the girl's ways were familial enough to bear recognition at least. It might be it was something to hold to.

Ahead, the grade of the interstate rose steeply for about an eighth of a mile, the road surface slick enough now that some cars were having trouble keeping traction. The light pickup just in front of Wayne skidded a little. Wayne stiffened but kept himself from touching his brakes. If nobody don't stop on the road, Wayne thought, if everybody just keeps going forward. He felt his own tires begin to slip and turned the steering wheel to and fro to keep enough forward momentum to continue climbing. It'd be something he'd have to teach to Ashton, how to drive on snow.

Of a sudden he wished to be out walking, out walking with the wind blowing, the snow blowing, out walking in the hills like when he was a boy, climbing up to the ridge tops, the snow up to his knees, weighing down the tree branches, falling down his coat collar. If they hadn't put the tree up yet at home, Wayne could volunteer to go cut it, maybe get Ashton to come along even. There were two or three little firs he remembered standing in the pasture from the year before. They'd be big enough now. They'd be perfect.

It was a cheerful thought, something to look forward to. For a while Wayne held in mind the fancy of him and Ashton taking an ax and cutting one of those pretty little fir trees and dragging it down off the pasture like Wayne used to do with his daddy. He began to plan it out in his mind, thinking where to find the ax, the rope for tying down the branches, wondering whether to take a sled to haul the tree on or just try and carry it between them. For a while he felt excited enough to forget a little his dread of the road. He began to think what a good Christmas it might be after all.

But then he came to dwell on the likeliness of the undertaking, the likeliness of Ashton trekking through the snow with him to search out and cut one of those little firs. She'd be more apt to object to the venture, more apt to throw a fit at the idea of cutting a tree even. If only we'd had another child or two, Wayne said to himself. If only we'd had another child that was a boy, a little boy that wanted to do things with his daddy. He shook his head, trying not to think along those lines, but the feeling of letdown had already commenced.

As they topped the rise and started down, Wayne thought he felt the car's rear tires begin to slip. He hit the brakes by reflex, and the car began to skid for real. Wayne kept calm enough to lay off the brakes and steer into the skid, but even so the car's rear end crossed over the line and into the oncoming lane. The lane was clear but for a coal truck just beginning the incline a few hundred feet away.

There was time enough for the driver to pull the truck off the road, though if the fellow did that, Wayne knew, he'd not be able to get enough momentum again to make the grade. He'd be stuck.

The truck barreled ahead, showing no sign even of slowing. Wayne tried to think what to do, but until the car quit its skid it was out of his control.

When he came within a car length, the coal truck driver gave a blast of his air horn, the sound so sudden in the quiet of the car that the three of them at once gave a shout of startlement. Smoothly then, its air horn still blaring, the truck veered onto the road shoulder. A spray of snow and muddy sludge spun off the big tires, striking the car's windshield, but there was no other contact.

Wayne got the car right again while it was still on the highway, maneuvering back across the slick-as-glass road surface to his own side again, aware the whole time of the demonstration he was providing for the whole line of travelers before and behind. See what that feller's mistake was? See what not to do?

Once he had the car straight in line again, Wayne found himself trembly and weak-feeling. The adrenaline had faded out of him, though his heart was thudding in such a way still to make him scared. He felt sick at his stomach, ill almost to the point of retching.

A trickle of sweat had started down his back. He thought for a moment about cracking the window to let in a little cold air. He wished he could shed his overshirt. He felt too tense, though, to let go the steering wheel even with one hand. He felt too tense even to take his attention from the road long enough to instruct Kharmin to lower the heater setting.

He saw the sign for the restaurant then, Ray and Betty's Kountry Kooking ½ Mile on Right. Of the twenty or so cars in direct view ahead, a third to a half had their blinkers on to turn off. For Wayne there was no question what to do. For the next half hour he skidded and slipped the half mile of downgrade with no further goal than arriving safe at Ray and Betty's gravel lot.

It was a shock getting out of the heated car. The wind was sharp enough to draw tears, the air so cold it was hurtful almost to breathe. They ducked their heads down, held their faces for protection in the crooks of their arms, and made for Ray and Betty's front door as best they could see it.

The dining area inside was so fully crowded there was scarce room even to stand. For a while the three of them lingered just inside the doorway. The one waitress, a woman in her fifties, maybe, with tightly curled hair tinted a bright shade of orange-red came winding toward them through the mob of stranded travelers. "There's no food left," she called, as in warning. "Come in and get warm. There's no food left, just coffee." She refilled an uplifted mug with what bitter dregs she had left to offer, then waved the emptied carafe at the bald-headed man behind the counter. "'Nother pot," she yelled.

They found standing space along a photograph-covered wall, squeezed in with the overflow of a dozen families. Wayne nodded to those crowded in at his shoulder and even said howdy to a couple of people as if he knew them, yet another old habit that came upon him south of the Mason-Dixon. It was funny that people seemed more familiar whenever he crossed back into his home state.

Kharmin and Ashton both stood with their shoulders hunched, leaning against Wayne's side as if to warm themselves. He felt the cold where they pressed against him. He felt them shivering. He hugged them and rubbed their arms to warm them. For a while then, Wayne began to feel better some. Being squeezed in elbow to elbow, his own little family with all these others, all heading somewhere home, had a cheering effect almost.

The fellow standing next to Wayne in his Cincinnati Reds ball cap, bright orange hunter's vest, and cowboy boots could have passed for a close cousin, he looked so much like family. Wayne felt a strong urge to speak to him. It was another of the things he missed about home, how easy you could get to talking with somebody, anybody, whether you knew them or not.

"Looks like we got some weather," Wayne said, smiling.

The fellow raised his cup of coffee and blew across the steam but made no response to show that he'd heard Wayne speak.

"We're coming from Dayton," Wayne said. "Going to Knott County. Where you headed to?"

The fellow took a cautious sip of his coffee, making a grimace as he swallowed. He glanced at Wayne, which gesture Wayne took as an inclination to talk.

"I dread this drive," Wayne said. "This time of year. I dread snow and ice worse than anything. Times I wonder if it's even worth it coming home."

The fellow took another sip of his coffee, and this time his expression was of outright annoyance. When he spoke his voice was harsh and pained-sounding, like someone with a bad sore throat. "You do what you have to," he croaked. His voice, raspy as it was, held the flattened-out strain of an accent more Ohio than Kentucky. He glared at Wayne and moved away toward the far end of the lunch counter where a small television set, turned to the Weather Channel, was bracketed to the wall.

Wayne watched the television screen for a while. The local forecast had come on, showing a radar map of the weather for a hundred-mile radius. The radar showed all clear to the north. Dead center of where they were, though, and on southward, the map showed an unbroken mass of red, the color for snow and sleet. He stared at the fellow he'd been talking to, stared at the back of his head. He wasn't that big-looking. Wayne figured he could take him if it came to it.

He held to that little bit of anger, focused in upon it. A damn Buckeye. He felt an oncoming surge of adrenaline, an urging to move, to do something, anything, so long as it wasn't sitting still. By god he'd not stay in this place, not if it come a blizzard. He felt a hand on his elbow and turned to see Kharmin and Ashton looking as if to speak.

"Ashton has a suggestion," Kharmin said.

"She does?" Wayne replied.

A flickering look, as of wariness or uncertainty, passed between Ashton and her mother. Wayne knew what was coming. He knew too what he'd have to say about it. He watched his daughter scuff her shoe against a spot of dark on the floor. He felt eager almost for the argument to commence.

Ashton didn't speak though. Instead, she pulled her coat tight about her and headed toward the entranceway. Wayne looked to Kharmin to explain, but she only smiled and placed her hand on his arm so as to hinder his following.

Ashton was several minutes gone. When she came back, her coat was unbuttoned and pulled around her so as to shield something she carried. She shrugged her coat off onto the floor, smiled toward her parents, and raised what she had brought in so that it could be viewed by the room.

It was a minute or two of people starting to take notice. Those nearest the entranceway turned first, their faces scowling as if in irritation of the cold let in. Then their senses took hold. Some one or two of them smiled. Others nudged their neighbors, taking meaningful sniffs and pointing. In a few minutes the whole roomful of them had hushed enough their ongoing chatter to take account of the girl standing there in the entranceway, holding in presentation a spiral-cut honey ham.

It took them awhile longer still to get in motion, for the idea of it to catch them all the way up. It was just one or two of those nearest the entranceway at first who'd got the fullest whiff and been made most mindful of how hungry they were, of how cheering it would be to eat, how fine to share in their eating. Soon, though, folks were standing throughout the room, pulling coats back on, finding car keys.

The young ones went laughing, hurrying against each other

out the doorway. The older folks proceeded politely, smiling one to another at their children's sudden high-spiritedness. Home-cooked platters of ham and turkey were retrieved, of green bean casseroles, of candied sweet potatoes, of cookies and cakes and pies, of rolls and biscuits. It was odd how quickly the feeling of sulkiness, of tension and worry and anger, even, that had filled up the room was overcome by the bounty of car trunks and backseats being turned out and shared around.

Wayne though felt something else come over him. The panicky feeling he'd been fighting against the day long came suddenly hard upon him. He tried to keep sight of the spiral-cut ham, but he lost it in a far corner amidst a gang of loud-talking teenage boys. They would arrive empty-handed, when they arrived, if they arrived. He slumped back against the wall, all at once sick at heart.

He tried again to conjure up the image of Christmastime he'd kept so constant in mind all these weeks now—his mom and dad, his brothers and sisters, their husbands and wives and children, all gathered happy and laughing around a table full of good food; the fireplace blazing with sweet-smelling spruce logs; outside a little snow coming down—but the vision was slow in coming and when it came it would not hold. Instead, what he came to dwell on was the aggravation of it all, the hard drive, the discomfort of having to share sleeping space with—of being hemmed in by, wherever you turned—this or that aunt or nephew or cousin, that truth be known were coming to be more strangers to him every year, so little he had to do with their lives.

The prospect of continuing on home seemed somehow wearisome beyond thought now. He ought to just give it up, he thought, give it up and head back to Ohio, back to Dayton. It would not be like the picture he held in his mind. It would not be like that at all.

He felt alone suddenly and realized that neither Ashton nor Kharmin were standing near to him. He looked and saw them with a group of other women acting as hostesses. For a moment he felt somehow spited. But then it occurred to him how satisfied they looked, how contented. He wondered if he was seeing it now, what his old mamaw claimed to recognize in Ashton's character, the semblance of his Aunt Reva.

He rose and went outside. The snow was falling heavily still, coming in squalls, the icy wind chilling him even through his coat. There was no traffic now, no seeing the highway hardly. Even the mountains were hidden in the blowing whiteness and the gloom of the early dark coming on.

He walked out into the parking lot. The plywood sign by Ray and Betty's nativity scene had fallen over, though the colored lights still burned and blinked. The message they spelled, Happy Birthday Jesus, could still be read.

Snow whipped about the Virgin Mary's kindly features. It piled upon the wise men's backs and shoulders, giving their figures the semblance of old men huddled against the cold. On its side in a growing drift by the holy infant's crib lay the figure of Joseph, the exposed face dirtied by a splatter of frozen sludge.

A sharp burning began in Wayne's nostrils. It occurred to him he might be taking a cold. He looked back toward the restaurant, watched through the frosted windows the movement of forms he could identify as neither strangers nor family. He could hear faintly, against the blast of wind, the sound of voices and maybe laughing. It could not be said how he felt.

# ALL THE ILLS

THE SIDEWALK IN FRONT of the Hazard Regional Hospital is strewn with cigarette butts. Some of the smokers are visitors, I grant you. But some wear gowns and robes. Some have drip bags hooked to their arms. They lean against those hat rack–looking carts, puffing away. The air is too still to clear the smoke. It hangs a few feet above their heads in a darksome cloud. What people won't do to theirselves.

They stand off a hair when I walk by. They nod and blow their smoke and watch me with side-turned eyes. The thought of their staring makes my neck itch. I catch myself swatting flies, feeling for bites. I can feel the sweat starting, running down my shirt collar, making a chill. I don't let on though. I'd as soon eat dirt as give these like the satisfaction.

I notice one old boy sitting on the steps with his head in his hands. He has a cast on his left wrist and two black eyes and a bandaged left ear. I know him for a Holyfield from Quicksand Creek that I used to take calls on the first Friday of every month. It'd be him drunk and falling down and dripping blood: Why, I sure hate you-all had to come all this way out here, and Now, I'll not lie to you, I have had some little to drink.

Then it'd be his old woman laying bunged up in the back room, her holding a butcher knife, cussing him in one breath and begging us not to take him off in the next. Oh, look what he done to me! and Oh, he's all I got! and Oh, he didn't go to! It's untelling which one would be worse off—her with her head stove in or him cut open—both too lit to feel it. And then it's Oh, my nerves! and Oh, my back! and Oh, this bad cough, it's like to kill me! And the younguns standing there taking it in, grinning like fools for the commotion, none but the littlest still with sense and shame enough to hide behind the furniture and cry. Lord have mercy!

I stand a minute on the steps and stare hard at him. He doesn't move a muscle, just holds his head and sucks his cigarette, the smoke rolling around his ears. But I know he's seen me. I know he knows I'm there. And I think, You better hang your head, you sorry trash. You better not look up.

The lobby is worse yet. It's all the ills of east Kentucky. Old folks with black lung. With crippling arthritis. With heart disease like Daddy has. It's what you'd expect from the lives they've led, the hard kind of work they've done, what they've made do with or without. Them you can feel for. But then too it's people my age with emphysema or liver disease from too much pills and smoking and drinking. And worse yet it's the young people. Some of these boys, and girls too, in here shot or stabbed or car-wrecked, or else putting on for the disability checks. Blissed-out on that methamphetamine. It's sick-making to look at them. It's television to blame and these sorry parents. And I blame the Welfare. I don't go to make no judgments though.

I pass among them, let them look me over—the haircut, the uniform jacket, the badge, the bulge of my holstered .38. Each step I take my stomach turns more sour. I want to be off alone on some far ridge top with clear air to breathe and nothing but trees around me.

I consider riding out Highway 15 to my house. I could surprise Angie and my little girl, maybe take us all out to Cliff Hagan's Steakhouse. It seems like a good idea until I think about it. Until I think about the reception I got last time. You're not supposed to come without calling. You're not supposed to come without calling.

Don't you think that made me hot? It nine going on ten in the morning and Angie standing there in that housedress still, barring the door. I told her it's my damn house whether I live there or not and I'll come and go as I please.

You're not supposed to come without calling. You're not supposed to come without calling. That whiny voice. Oooh, I'd liked to smacked her. I feel a burning in my chest, and I have to tell myself, "No, Brody. You're doing yourself no good."

Daddy's room is on the third floor, down the hall from Intensive Care. I pass by the elevators in favor of the stairs, and by the time I've walked up I feel calm again. I need to tell Daddy I've fed his dogs and put out hay for his cattle and that one old mule he keeps and made sure there's water for everything.

I see Katrina the minute I step into the hallway. She looks so much like Mommy it's a shock to me. She's standing outside Daddy's room wiping her eyes with a tissue, her and that husband of hers, that Pete, and two of her younguns, I can't even name them for sure. And there's half a dozen of that church crowd with them—Betty Goble and Marvin Justice and that Viola Owens. The Trace Fork Church of Zion. You can't catch a cold without them putting you on the prayer list. I'd about forgot about Daddy rededicating himself to the Lord. I'd about put it out of my mind.

My first thought is to sneak off before I'm spotted, but before I can, Katrina spots me. Standing there talking to Pastor Justice, Katrina's all tears and meekness, her cheeks red as apples. But when she sees me, it's like a switch being thrown. Her face cools. She crosses her arms on her chest and rolls her eyes like Oh, Lord give me strength. There's never no mistaking Katrina's feelings.

I have no choice. I march right up, put my arm around her shoulders, and say, "Hello, stranger."

"Stranger, yourself," she tells me. But then she hugs me and says, "God bless." The way she says it, I believe I'd just as soon been told to go burn in hell. It's a wonder her tongue don't break off in her head.

"Where's the rest of the clan?" I ask. "Where's Johnny? Where's Missy and her bunch?"

She doesn't answer, just sighs and shakes her head. But I never expected no more answer. I know where they're at, our brother and sister. Off trying to decide whether they love Daddy more or hate him. I don't say it.

"I reckon Daddy's had a time," I say.

Her face peakens. Her eyes mist over. "It's a pity," she says. "Lord love its heart. Laying there in sickness." She dabs her eyes with her wadded tissue.

"He's a tough one," I say.

"We've been praying for him," she says.

"Well I know he appreciates it."

"The prayer of the upright is the Lord's delight," she says. She pauses to slip the tissue into her dress pocket. When she looks at me again her eyes are dry and stern. "Of course they's a many we've prayed for and it not took. A many that have backslid and forsooken vows and turned deaf ears to the Lord's good word."

I think a minute about what she said and how she meant me to take it. There's any number of cutting replies I could make. About that husband of hers. About them kids. And Katrina's not above reproach her own self. But then I say to myself, "No, Brody. What's the use?"

I just smile. "I know it's told in his recovery," I say. "Your-all's prayers. It's the Lord's blessing you-all being here."

She frowns and makes to shoo me off, but her face has reddened a little. I know I've hit her where she lives. I go off down the hall while she's still yet wondering about my sincerity.

I get a cup of coffee in the cafeteria and sit at a corner table to wait. It's not hardly noontime yet. I've been up since a quarter till five and already it feels like the day will never be gone. The older I get it seems like the earlier I rise. Daddy used to say he'd got to where he was rising up almost before he laid down. His legs bothered him, sciatica and arthritis. It's a blessing I don't have no more wrong with me than this heartburn. It's coffee kills me. But I won't give up my coffee.

The dinner crowd increases as a quarter after comes on. I see that Miller boy come in as I'm getting up to leave. I know all about his troubles, about his wife's baby coming too early and there being complications and them not able to go home yet. He's wearing his uniform, so I know he's just come in from patrol. He's a young-looking man still, the most of his hard duty still yet before him.

My first term in office, I did stops on drunk drivers and speeders. I did traffic control at high school ball games. I headed up funeral processions. Once in a while I went in with the DEA or the state police to burn out a pot patch or arrest somebody dealing out of their home, but it was mostly boresome.

Even so I'd come home and tell Angie how rough I had it. Oh, it's such a trial. I don't believe I can take it, the way people are. She'd rub my neck and say, Poor baby. The truth is I was just putting on.

Then I got my first bad case. It was this young high school girl that got abducted. We found her half a mile up a holler, raped and beat to death. From the way her face looked . . . I got sick that day.

We found who done it sitting parked in a creek bed not far from the scene. I remember his face and eyes were bloody from where she'd gouged him with her fingernails. There was blood and filth on his clothes and on the interior of his pickup. I remember it was a green Chevy with a camper top and a trout sticker on the tailgate. He never made no protest when we took him, never made no sign we were even there until one of the deputies slipped and fell in the creek, and then he laughed. Him just killed a girl and able to laugh at somebody falling in mud. No more conscience than a cur dog.

As I walk by the Miller boy's table, I put my hand on his shoulder and squeeze. He looks up at me. He's not been in uniform a full year. He knows me, but not so well as to be familiar.

Next week I'll slip an envelope in his mailbox, seventy-five or a hundred, whatever I can scrape up. He won't know who did it, not directly, but he'll remember that he saw me in the hospital and that I was respectful to him and concerned. It ain't because he's a state police. It ain't because he's a Miller and his family can carry half of

Clear Creek at election time. I'll do it because of what kind of fix he's in, because it's a way to behave. I don't have no ulterior motives.

The church crowd is gone by the time I wind back around to Daddy's room. It's just Katrina now, hovering about the doorway, wiping her eyes. I just nod and go on in the room. He's laying in his bed so still you'd think he was asleep if not dead. His eyes are open, though, and blinking. He's lost so much weight I almost wonder if it's him laying there. His arms are sticks. His body's just a wrinkle in the sheets.

I call, How are you? He doesn't answer or move. The back of his left hand is laid across his forehead. His right hand is pressed palm down on an open Bible, one finger pointing, like he's marking a line for reading.

I step into the room. "Daddy," I say. "It's Brody?"

He lowers his arm to cover his eyes, but still he doesn't speak. I look at the bedpan on the side table, at the monitors reading out how much life he has in him. It's so quiet in the room I can hear the air whistling through his nose tube.

"I got the rest of your hay in," I say. "I've watered and fed."

He looks up then, but not at me. His eyes are moist like he's been crying. "I ain't doing no good," he says. His voice is so weak I can barely hear him.

"I got the rest of your hay in," I say again.

"It's God's love struck me down," he says. "Struck me down in my arrogance."

I wonder at the change in him. Two weeks ago we were mowing hay together. His biggest complaint was being tired and out of breath. It's not just his health he's lost but his nerve. And I wonder if it's his illness or the church that's robbed him most.

"I had that Sizemore boy come in and trim that old jenny's hooves," I say. I move close to the bed, leaning down to put my hand on the bed rail. It's raised so he won't fall out on the floor in his weakness. His eyes focus on my chest. "They were growed out so much she couldn't hardly walk," I say.

He gives a start, like he's just now seeing me. I watch the sense come back into his face. After a moment he nods weakly. "I thank you," he says, and I know it's something like his old self I'm talking to again.

We speak of weather and livestock and the chores left waiting him at home. Katrina comes in after a while, though she stands close to the doorway still. The look on her face is pure misery. I can't help but feel the least bit kindly to her. Her and me are the only ones that didn't take sides against him years ago. I give her that.

I'm not laying no blame on Missy or brother John. Lord knows I don't fault Mommy for leaving out. She'd had enough of his meanness, more than enough. But I never could hold him in complete account for how he acted. It was what-all he'd went through. Korea. When he was drinking, he used to recall it all to us, Mommy and us children, gather us around and describe how a man's body would look after he'd been dead awhile, how it would swell and turn black and burst open, how it would smell. He'd tell about boys close as brothers getting killed right next to him, shot or blowed up or burned alive. He'd talk about how many he killed and what way he killed them. We'd set there and listen, afraid to move lest he bare his hand. Of course it may be he'd have drunk like he did no matter what.

When I make to leave he offers his hand to shake. I try and be gentle when I take it. It's cold and bloodless-looking and trembly. I feel the least bit ill touching it. He looks at me funny for a second. I start to smile, but then I see the look come on his face, the look I know well, the look that says he's about to knock fire out of me. It's funny how I feel for a second, almost like I wish he would, but there's barely enough strength left in him to raise his head, or enough will either. I squeeze his hand, shaking it for real, squeeze until his knuckles pop. I manage to leave without saying anything more. At least I've got that much sense.

All up and down the hall are patients' rooms, some with doors standing open. I hear low moans, some weeping. I try not to look in. I'm thirsty, but the first fountain I pass has a tobacco cud clogging the drain. I feel myself start to shake. Just the sight of that foulness makes me want to tear hell out of whatever I can put my hands on.

By the time I get down to the lobby, I'm so mad I can't hardly see straight.

For some reason I think about the times—there's been a few—when I've gone on calls to the houses of people I've knowed. I'd go in and see piled-up trash or beer cans strewed on the floor or half-gone bottles of liquor or pills. It's embarrassing is what it is, going in on somebody you're used to seeing out in their garden every day or at the grocery store or the barber's and finding out how bad-off in truth they really are. It's disheartening.

It's something like that feeling I got seeing Daddy in that bare, scrubbed room with an oxygen tube clipped to his nostril and a feeder tube in the vein of his arm. I feel myself getting mad at him, like him laying there is through some fault of his own. That don't make no sense, I know. It ain't no crime being sick in the hospital.

I think about Angie telling me I couldn't see nothing but the bad in people. Even if that's so, who is she to say it? The time she brought that church crowd to our house. To pray for our union. To bring God's counsel to our union. I only regret I left out that night. I only regret I didn't throw them each one out a window. My own damn house.

I head for a pay phone. That child is as much mine as hers, I think. I've still got some rights in her regard. Something funny happens when I pick up the phone. I can't think of my own number. I press the coin return. Drop the change into the slot once more. I tap the three-number prefix, then stop. I don't know whether to laugh or cuss. Who forgets their own phone number?

I stand holding the receiver so long my ear gets numb. I begin to think about who-all has handled it before me, about who-all has breathed onto the mouthpiece. When I move it away I see the oily smear of thumbprints on the black plastic. I'm about sick to my stomach when I finally get my memory again. I repeat the number to myself as I dial. I listen to the rings. I count up to twelve before I finally hang up. I know she's there. I know she's not answering of a purpose. She knows it's me calling.

I walk outside among the smokers. I see that Holyfield still sitting on the steps, his ride not come yet. I stare at the back of his neck, rattle the change in my pocket. His head bends almost to his ankles, like me just standing there is a weight pressing him down. And then he does something I don't expect. He looks up at me, looks me straight in the eye, like he's about to tell me something.

Of a sudden then his cigarette drops and sparks against the sidewalk. He hops up and jake-legs it down the sidewalk, shaking his head in a way that makes me want to go after him and ask what it is he thinks he means. These others all stare at me now, and I'm glad of my polished shoes, my uniform jacket, my badge.

I'm in my pickup and driving out Highway 15 before I even realize where I'm headed. My brain is spinning. Is it too much to ask? Some more understanding? After what-all I give her, is it too much to expect? Some more consideration? She never wanted, nor our baby neither, not for a blessed thing. For her to up and leave me like she did. Not no more consideration of me than a dog.

Just before the turnoff to my house, I make myself pull off onto the road shoulder. I'm wound up still, thinking what I'd like to say to Angie, what I'd like to do. It's an effort to hold myself still, to try and think calm. I shut the pickup off. There's so little traffic this time of morning I can hear the creek running nearby. I tell myself I have to think what is it that really matters here.

I think about Daddy living out these last years as alone as he's been, half his children not speaking to him. I'm not near as old as he was when Mommy left out. I ain't a fool. I see the path I'm on. I see where it is I'm headed.

I think about Angie. It's heartbreaking to me now to think how close we once were. We just need to calm down. We just need to look at things in a different light. Ain't no problem don't have a solution. If I could just sit down with her, explain things to her the way I have it lined out in my mind. I ain't saying I never done her wrong. I ain't saying that. But I ain't a bad man. I ain't a bad man at heart. I can change my ways. I can change my ways and I will.

For some reason I think about my baptism, those solemn witnesses lining the creek bank, waiting to shout and sing at the moment of my salvation. I remember still being head under in that mucky water, coming up for my first breath as a member of the body of Christ. My soul saved, my sins washed clean for good and all. I listen to the creek running. I think about that good feeling I once had, thinking I was saved, thinking I was redeemed. I feel myself start to calm.

By the time I start the pickup again, I've figured what I need to say. I feel better driving the little distance up the branch road. Things seem better now that I've reasoned it out. I pause a minute after I pull in the driveway. I notice how rutted it is from where the gravel has washed away. What it needs is paving. It's something I should have done long ago. I look the place over. It occurs to me how the yard could be leveled and made bigger with a couple hours' dozer work. There'd be room enough, maybe, for a deck or a brick patio. I could put in a gazebo at the far end like Angie always wanted. A grape arbor even. It's a wonder to me I've not done all this before. This could be a showplace. I could come home of a night and get my tension out doing improvements.

I walk by the Taurus I bought new last year and that Angie got in the settlement. I start to get mad when I notice how grimed over it is with tree sap and road grit. Then I tell myself it's just a car. It don't mean a thing. The fact I'm still making payments on it don't mean a thing. Angie does the best she can. I walk toward the house, thinking generous thoughts.

Angie flings the door open before I can even knock. What I want is to hug her and tell her how pretty she is and how much I've missed the sight of her, despite all. But I can't get the words out. I can't speak. All I can do is stand there, looking surly, I know.

"Well?" she asks.

Something flares up in me at the sound of her voice. I feel a little gurgle deep in my stomach. I taste something sour at the back of my throat. I feel myself getting mad again. I try to keep calm as I answer. What comes out, comes out wrong. "It's nice to see you too," I say.

The skin draws so tight across her forehead I can see the veins standing out at the temples. Her jawline bunches up with muscle. Her teeth flash. And her eyes. It's a look of pure hatred she gives me with her eyes. And then she starts in with that mouth. It's Who do you think you are, barging into my house? and What do you think you're about, I'd like to know? and Yip, yip-yip, yip-yip, on and on.

Then it's her bringing up all her old complaints and me bringing up mine and her screaming at me and me screaming at her. I don't know how long it is before I get hold of myself again. Shut up, I tell myself. Just shut up. She winds down pretty soon. It takes two to argue. In a little while she's done.

I take my chance to speak, keeping my voice low and calm, like I would if I was on a call. I catch myself almost calling her ma'am. "I apologize," I say. "I'm sorry. I shouldn't have come without calling. I'm sorry. I know I'm in the wrong." I say that again and again, studying her as I speak.

"I'm not asking for nothing," I say. "Not a thing. I don't deserve nothing and I'm not asking. You don't have to worry about me being after something. I'm not."

I pause to take a breath, to get my words in order. "This situation we're in," I say, "I know it's me that's brought us to it. I know it. It's on me. I know it."

For a minute then she looks at me, like Who is this talking? But her face has softened a little, and I know I've struck a chord. I start to feel myself taking charge. I feel like I know just what to say. "What I come out here for . . . what I mean to say . . . I've thought through some things is all. Believe it or not. I've thought through and I've prayed and I've come to realize some things."

Of a sudden she stiffens up. "If you expect—" she starts.

I lower my voice still more. "I don't expect a thing," I say. "Not a thing. All I'm saying is I want to do better. I want to do right. That's all. That's it. This situation we're in, it's on me. I don't expect a thing. I don't have no delusions."

I pause. I tell myself Be careful. You've said enough now. Be careful.

"That's all I want to say. That's what I come out here for. I love you. I still do. I love that little girl of ours and I love you. I'm always going to. That's all I mean to say." And I hush.

For a minute we stand there staring at one another. She doesn't say anything, but I know I've struck a chord. I know I've got through to something. She'll be thinking about my words, turning them over to find some hidden intent. She'll doubt me being sincere. I've laid the foundation though.

I spy my daughter as I start to leave. She's standing a few feet behind her mother. It's not been a week since I've seen her, but she seems more grown even in that little time. I have to fight myself not to try and speak to her. I know I can't though. Not right now, I can't. I can't undo myself, not now. I make myself leave.

I drive fast out Highway 15. I feel good. It's like I've been dashed in the face with a bucket of cold water. I feel like I've started on a new path. I know it. In my heart I know it. It's like I've come awake somehow.

The pickup starts to fishtail before I even realize how fast I'm going. I drift into a curve. The steering wheel bucks in my hands. I hold the road but come into the following straight stretch on the wrong side of the line, head-on to some old car. I cut hard, hear my tires screech, feel my outside wheels lift from the pavement. I brace for the smack, but then the pickup gives a lurch and somehow I'm four wheels down again and passing the car on my own side of center.

My hands are still gripping hard to the steering wheel when I come to rest on the road shoulder. I sit for a minute while the adrenaline flows out of me. When my heart has slowed a little, I get out and walk around the pickup. There's no damage that I can see, no sign of any mishap, none but my shaking knees. I get back behind the wheel and start to go on. Then something occurs to me. That car. It occurs to me that I know that old car.

I sight my objective two minutes after I begin pursuit. Before he even sees me coming, I'm up hard on his bumper. He slows some but doesn't pull off. It's not until I reach to turn on the siren and don't find the switch that I remember I'm not in my cruiser. I trail him another five miles like that, then turn off behind him onto Quicksand Creek. A mile further when the blacktop road changes to dirt, I flash my headlights and lay on with my horn.

He pulls over. He don't know to do anything else. I count the crowd of heads in the car. It's old Holyfield driving and next to him a young kid and then his old woman and then an older boy and girl in the backseat. Holyfield stares at me in his side mirror as I walk up. He rolls the window down but doesn't get out. He's waiting for me to speak.

"I want to talk to you," I say.

"What is it I done?" he asks.

That gets me. Him questioning me. "Just get out of the damn car," I say.

I reach through the open window and collar him and jerk the door open. He holds on to the steering wheel for a second, but I tumble him out. He hits the ground like a sack of wet manure, then grabs hold of my leg. "Get up," I say. I slap him to get him to turn loose, but he just holds on tighter.

"Get up from there," I hear myself shout, though my voice sounds far off. There's a dull little pain starting at the back of my head. I feel myself getting sick. It's the smell of him—his unwashed hide, the cigarette smoke in his clothes. It's what it reminds me of. A call to Jones Fork for a burned-out trailer—the smell of fabric burning and wood and smoldering metal, of bodies broiling in among melted-together plastic and glass and insulation.

I punch Holyfield in the head with my closed fist. Go easy, I tell myself, but it's like my brain and body are in two separate places. Holyfield ducks his head between his shoulders, and I think here's a man used to getting beat. I punch him again, on his shoulder, on the crown of his skull, but despite all, the memories rise up on me. That car crash on Beaver Creek—the one boy smeared across the pavement like a dead dog, the other mangled up inside the wreckage so bad you couldn't hardly tell skin and bone apart from metal.

That child on Black Mare . . . What Angie couldn't never understand. What nobody couldn't never understand. It's how the job wears on a man. A law officer is human like anybody else.

When I come to myself, Holyfield is curled up on the ground, and I'm standing astraddle him. I swear it looks like he's grinning at me. Grinning.

I leave him laying there. I'm not mad anymore. I feel weak and sore-muscled. It's a chore just to haul myself into the cab of my pick-up. Let's go, I tell myself. Let's go. But the more I try to will myself to drive on, the more I just want to sit still. I think about that look he give me at the hospital. I intend to know what he meant by that.

I'm doing myself no good, I know it. I close my eyes and press my forehead against the steering wheel. I try to think about something else. That last day I worked outside with Daddy. I remember the heat of the morning, the itch of crumbled straw and seed heads in my clothes, the smell of the hay rising in dust clouds off the bales. For a second I have that day in mind. Then I lose it to thoughts of Daddy being sick and in the hospital.

I open my eyes. Holyfield is on his feet again, staring at me, not moving. Get on! I want to shout, Get! Instead, I step out of the truck. I strip off my sheriff's jacket, my badge, unclip my .38, and lay them wrapped together on the seat. I'm surprised at how much lighter I feel. Holyfield's family is out of the car now. They stand distant, quiet and staring.

Oh sure, now. I'm not fool enough to believe that we can resolve our differences with just a snap of the fingers. Oh no. It will take work between the two of us. Real work. I think about Angie, how much older she looked to me in just a week's time.

The bandage on Holyfield's head is dripping, and there's a ring of stick burrs in his hair. His face is bruised and dirt-smeared. The one eye that's not swollen shut is raised to look at me.

I flex my hands. They have begun to swell. I force my fingers closed, throw a punch to the side of Holyfield's head. I feel a knuckle crack, the pain like a charge of electricity up and down my arm. I punch again with my hurt fist, and for an instant I feel myself relieved of care.

Holyfield doubles up on the ground. I kick him in the ribs with my boot toe, but there's no satisfaction in that. I want to break my hands on him. I want to gouge his eyes out with my thumbs. I grab his hair, pull his head back. I pop short punches at his cheek, at his ear—whatever shows for a target. I don't know how long it is I beat him. It's like hoeing corn or mowing hay. You get into it good you can lose all track of yourself.

# NEW-USED

MARK'S MOTHER AND SISTER sat bowed over the sewing machine in the corner furthest from the TV, his mother speaking softly while his sister aligned the edges of two pieces of scrap cloth beneath the machine needle. The baby sat beneath their chairs, pulling dress material and folded patterns from the bags of sewing his mother had taken in. When the scrap cloth was in place, Mark's mother lowered the needle and pressed the foot pedal that his sister's legs were too short to reach still. The little motor whirred, drowning the sound of the TV and turning the picture to jagged lines.

Mark watched his sister move the pieces of scrap cloth beneath the flickering needle as the thread bobber spun atop the housing. For a moment he was struck by the way she rested her elbows on the machine cabinet, how she held her chin raised and squinted her eyes, her face shadowed by the slanting light of the single overhead bulb. Watching her, he let his eyes go out of focus, the way he looked at clouds sometimes or distant trees until their forms blurred and turned to different shapes. But then his mother let off the foot pedal and raised the needle. The thread bobber stilled, and in the sudden quiet, whatever different shape he'd been about to make of his sister, he lost. He watched her pick up the scissors. They were large and awkward in her hand, and it took her two tries to catch the thread between the blades.

Mark's father came from the back room then, his steps so light upon the bare-wood flooring that Mark was almost startled to see him among them. He was dressed in the dark pants and white shirt he wore on weekends. Even so, he looked like a man readying himself more for work than town—the cuffs of his shirt rolled above his wrists, his pants pockets bulging with keys and knife and billfold, a fresh smear of oil already marking the knuckles of his right hand.

He shut off the TV, and for a moment the only sound was the slight rasp of paper as he sorted through a stack of envelopes. When he spoke, his voice seemed sudden and too loud in the small room. "Betty," he said, "I can't find the car title."

For a moment more his mother sat studying the practice seam his sister had run in the scrap cloth. Then she rose from the sewing machine.

They stood quietly facing each other, and Mark wondered if the argument they'd been having was about to rise between them again. It had been a month since his father had gotten on operating an end loader at Birchfield Coal, and it had been a month since he'd begun to speak of trading cars. Each day he'd knocked and banged on the old Ford, cussing and declaiming. "This old rattletrap, it's burning oil. This old rattletrap, it's costing me more to keep up than it's worth."

His mother the whole month had argued without speaking, saying neither yes nor no in words, just holding her head in such a way, like a person saying a prayer or like a person adding something in her head. Finally she'd said may as well. "May as well now, while we can." His father had fallen silent then, and from then on crept quietly about the house, his face stiff and guilty-looking.

As he spoke this morning, Mark heard the growing agitation in his voice, saw in the growing redness of his face how he thought himself questioned again, questioned on this move he'd come hard to and was not sure of.

"I've got to have something to drive."

"I'm not saying nothing."

"How am I going to work if don't have something to drive?"

"I'm not saying nothing."

"I've got to have something to drive." He spoke slowly, his spread hands measuring out the words. "It's as simple as that."

His mother stood with her shoulders stooped, her head bent forward like she was peering downward at some work in hand, and the expression on her face again was of somebody adding something in her head. But suddenly the look on her face changed. She nodded her head as if she'd come to some agreement. Then she took a pair of envelopes from her dress pocket and handed both to his father. "Can you stop at the store?" she asked.

The envelope with the car title he stuck in his shirt pocket. The other, with the booklet of WIC vouchers and the grocery list, he held loosely in his hand as if he didn't know what to do with it. "Do we still need these," he asked.

"We still do," she said.

"Can't I just take you later?"

Mark's mother said nothing more, and after a moment his father's face began to cool, the redness fading to his ear tips and cheeks. He looked with lowered eyes about the room, and soon a scattering of pinkish splotches on the back of his neck was all that showed of his worry. "I don't care to do it," he said, his voice so soft that he might have been speaking to himself. "I hate using these vouchers, is all." He folded the envelope with the list and vouchers and stuffed it deep into his back pocket.

Mark rose to follow his father out the door, and as he glanced over his shoulder he saw his mother sitting again next to his sister at the sewing machine. Their elbows were propped together upon the cabinet, their heads lowered so that they were eye level with the machine needle, their chins pointing. His mother's shoulders seemed not to slump now but to curve to her work in a way that gave her ease, and his sister's shoulders curved in the selfsame way. Beneath their chairs, the baby lay happily tangled in a yard of paisley cloth, a spool of black thread clutched in her hand.

The old Ford fired on the first spark, the engine rumbling loudly as they backed out of the yard. It was just a six cylinder, and it was just the manifold being rusted through that made it so loud. Even so, Mark loved the sound. He loved the feel of the engine vibrating through the floorboard, up through his feet and legs and into his belly, and he loved the gassy smell of exhaust.

It was cool enough in the morning now to tell that fall was coming, though the trees on the high ridges had not begun to brown and the days were still running long into the evenings. As they drove past the garden, Mark noticed how picked over everything looked. The sweet corn and beans and tomatoes had all been canned and put in the basement for winter. The lettuce was gone, and what onions were left had flower heads topping the blades. There were still sweet potatoes to be dug, though, and a few hard cabbage heads to be pulled. And the half-dozen apple trees scattered at the garden's edges were still full of fruit. Over the next week or two they'd pick apples. Mark would get to sell a few bushels by the roadside, though most of what they picked they'd peel and quarter for freezing. In the wintertime they'd have apples for making fried pies and stack cakes.

The road was paved, but it was narrow and followed the twisting path of the Auglin Branch of Troublesome Creek. Small houses and trailer homes sat on either side. About every fourth or fifth place was run down, the yards strewn with garbage and rusted-out old cars and tossed-off appliances and junked furniture. The other places, though, were well kept up, neatly painted or sided, the yards mown and laid out with fruit trees and flowering bushes; those with room enough had garden plots and sheds or barns for tillers and tools or the livestock that was kept more for pastime than need.

Whenever they passed someone out in his yard or met another vehicle, Mark's father would raise his hand from the steering wheel, and the other person would raise his hand too. They drove past the gas-company well on the little bottom where Hubbard Martin pastured his horses and started up the incline of Auglin Mountain. Halfway up, the overhang of timber thickened so much that the sun broke through only in scant patches, and the shadowed road steepened so that Mark's father had to drop the old Ford into first gear to keep it moving.

At the mountain's crest on a topmost rise of rocky ground just off the road sat the Gipson place. Half-a-dozen times that summer, Mark's father had caught the various children filling sacks in his garden. "I swear I'd give them a poke of apples now and again," he'd say each time after chasing them out. "I'd give them a peck of beans now and then if they'd just ask and not steal. Some people don't know how to act, is all."

The house sat propped on a set of half-toppled creek-stone pillars and leaned so crookedly that even looking up you could see the perch of the swaybacked roof and the black smear of soot around the chimney. There was a high porch going around three sides, piled underneath with loose stacks of gray lumber and old car tires.

A set of bedsprings leaned against a stone well box. Two old cars sat rusting in the weeds beyond a smokehouse. On the smokehouse door were nailed half-a-dozen greasy skin boards, some still holding tattered bits of dried animal hide. The yard itself was stony and bespoiled of grass and strewn with tin cans and bottles and other odd bits of trash, like the leavings of a high flood.

As they passed, Mark saw two of the older Gipson boys come out of the house. They were lanky, big boys, with shaggy heads of uncombed hair and misfitting clothes—a too-large shirt on one, a too-small pair of britches on the other. They stood on the porch with their hands on their hips, staring, and there was something in the shifty, needful looks of their faces that left Mark feeling hostile toward them even after they'd crested the mountain and were out of sight of the house on the other side.

When they passed the Auglin Church of Christ, his father said, "Your mommy worries a way too much." He gunned the engine then, and the car lurched ahead, gaining speed. When they crossed the bridge at the intersection with 1068 and hit the little bit of downgrade, the car was going fast enough to rise free of the pavement.

Mark felt his stomach fall and made to grab hold of the door handle and brace his feet against the dash, but before he could they were touched down again. He heard his father begin to laugh, and Mark laughed too as the thrill of what they'd just done came full over him.

"That's just between you and me," his father said. "All right?"

"All right," Mark said.

They left the old Ford parked by the showroom and walked down a short grade past the garage to the back lot. When they came to the used cars, Mark's father paused for a moment, his face excited and happy-looking. Then he cut across to the next-to-last row and strode quickly toward the far end, the cars getting older and more rundown the further back they went.

Halfway down he stopped before a green Dodge pickup. It was a short-bed with a sliding back window and a pinstripe trim decal running along the sides from the hood to the tailgate. At first sight Mark thought the Dodge looked at least as old as their Ford. The trim decal had peeled some and the paint along the doors and fenders was bubbled in spots, though no rust showed through yet. The bed was so used-looking you could see bare metal where the paint had worn off, and the tailgate seemed bent slightly, as if it had been backed into something while open.

"There it is," his father said. "It's not been sold." He walked around the pickup, running his hands over the wheel wells and body panels. He looked at the tires. He opened the hood and felt the hoses and belts. Then he knelt to look at the pavement beneath the engine.

"That's it," he said. "It's what I've been looking at." He studied the Dodge a moment more, then turned and looked toward the showroom. A few salesmen paced about behind the big plate-glass window. Others stood on the front lot talking to customers across the hoods of the new models. None had hurried out to greet them when they pulled in, and none was bothering with them now.

"I believe I'm going to have to sell myself this vehicle," Mark's father said. He smiled. "Wait here," he said. Then he winked at Mark and walked off toward the showroom.

When he was sure that no one was looking, Mark slipped behind the steering wheel. For a moment he sat studying the interior. The vinyl of the dash was split open and curled up in a couple of places, and though the upholstery was still good, the bench seat sagged a little on the driver's side. The truck was not new, but it was not beat to death either; you could tell somebody had kept it up good. It had been a man like his father, probably, who'd owned it last—a big, heavy man to sag the seat like that, who knew how to work with tools and who liked to do his own repairs probably. Mark gripped the steering wheel with both hands and imagined the sound of the motor revving, of the tires scratching against pavement. He was far along in his pretend driving when he heard the sound of his father's voice.

He stood nearby again, talking to a salesman now. The man looked like he might have been as old as Mark's father, but he was slimmer, with a fuller head of hair that was combed straight back from his forehead as neat as if it had just been barbered. He wore a white shirt and a tie but no jacket, and he had a small mustache as neat and trim as his haircut.

"That's it," Mark's father said. "That's the one I'm looking at."

The salesman stood distant at first, staring back toward the new-model lot as if he might hear someone calling him. After a moment he shrugged and said, "All right. Which one is it, you say?"

"That green Dodge," Mark's father said. "They's the least bit of Bondo in them wheel wells."

The salesman shrugged. "That's a package," he said mildly. "It's got that 318 V-8 engine, A/C, Goodyear all-weather radials, power brakes, power steering, AM/FM cassette if I'm not mistaken. It's a wonder it's still on the lot." He touched his mustache and looked over his shoulder toward the front lot again.

"Them rear tires are wore down some," Mark's father said.

"That's truck's been kept up good," the dealer said. "Still plenty of miles in it. Be good for a work truck or a play truck either one."

"What's that leaking there under the crankcase?"

"Well I'd imagine it's oil," the salesman said. "A vehicle ten years old is going to have some drips." He smiled. "Did you say you were looking to buy or just looking?"

Mark's father flushed red in the face. "I've got three hundred cash to put down," he said. "Plus my trade-in. Now, what's the book on this Dodge?"

"That your trade-in?" the salesman asked. He glanced toward the front lot where the Ford was parked. The evening before, Mark had helped his father wash and wax her, vacuuming out the seats, wiping the dash and steering wheel and instrument panel, even cleaning the rubber floor mats. They had polished the bumpers and grill and cleaned off the bugs and road tar with gasoline. As a last touch Mark's father had gone around dipping an old toothbrush into a mug of cold coffee and scrubbing a shine onto the black-wall tires. When they finished they'd stood back to admire their work, and Mark's father had said, "I ought to just keep her."

But as Mark looked at the Ford now with the salesman standing by, all he could think was how shabby it looked. It didn't look like anything anybody would want to buy, not if they had any choice in the matter.

"You don't want to keep it for a fishing car?" the salesman asked.

Mark's father didn't speak. There was a look on his face almost of pain, like something in his belly was hurting him. He turned away as if he had not heard the salesman's question.

The salesman looked at Mark. He winked. "We'll give you something for it," he said. He smiled again and slapped Mark's father on the shoulder. "Let's walk up to the office and see if we can't put you in that Dodge. You got a clear title on that Ford, then? No lien?"

---

Mark's father was quiet for a long while after they pulled out of the car lot. He drove the Dodge with both hands on the steering wheel, leaning so far forward that his back didn't touch the seat. Finally, after a few miles, he cleared his throat and in a stiff-sounding voice said, "How are you doing in school?"

"All right, I reckon," Mark said.

His father tilted his head as if to hear better. Mark tried to think of something else to tell, but it was a punishment to find what to say. He began to wish they were both somewhere else. He wished they were both out in the garden with a patch of corn to hoe or the tiller motor to fix so they could have some task to talk over. He wished they were not just riding along in the pickup his father had just traded for, both of them feeling less good for some reason than they should be. When after a minute Mark said nothing more, his father cleared his throat again and turned away.

As they neared the grocery his father slowed the pickup and put on the blinker. But just as they seemed about to pull into the parking lot, he touched the gas again and they went on by. "Something up here I want to you to see," he said.

They drove fast on the twisty, narrow road, hardly slowing even for the sharp curves. A few miles further, they turned off the highway onto an unnamed access road that was not paved and so badly rutted the pickup had to be steered side to side to keep traction.

Near the top of the hill, they drove through a bar gate and onto the Birchfield Coal strip site. They drove slowly along the row of workers' personal vehicles, almost all of them four-wheel drive trucks or Jeeps and almost all of them newer than the Dodge. For a while, then, they parked and watched the operation—the heavy equipment running across the five-acre ledge sheared from the ridgeline.

Some of the equipment was so large—the rock trucks and bucket loaders—that the men operating them could as well have been taken for machine parts as people. Mark's father pointed to an end loader working to fill a line of Mack trucks. The machine scooped and filled without ceasing, its path so unchanging that it seemed to leave only a single set of tread marks between the coal banks and truck beds. "That's what I run," Mark's father said. He raised his hand as if to wave to the small figure on the distant machine. "That's Jack Burrell on there. He's operated one of them things for thirty years. I've been on it a month and I feel like a old man. I go to bed at night with my teeth still rattling."

After a while a small group of men came walking from the direction of the coal face. They carried lunch boxes and large water jugs and were a long time crossing the field. When they were near enough, Mark's father blew the pickup's horn. A slim, older-looking man paused and looked their way, then started toward them. A shorter man with a large belly and a shaggy beard followed.

"Let's get out here and speak with these fellers," Mark's father said.

"Boys, I'm a-tell you what," the bearded man said as he came near.

"It's not new exactly," Mark's father said.

"New to you."

"New to me," Mark's father agreed.

Mark stood out of the way while his father and the two men gathered around the pickup's raised hood. He watched them searching over the engine with their coal-blackened hands, and for a moment he worried that they might find something wrong with the truck, something that his father should have seen but had not.

He stared for a moment at the ram's-head hood ornament, then ran his gaze all over the truck, following the line of the trim from the front grill to the rear bumper. From all he could see the Dodge was a clean, solid truck, well kept up, not new but as close to it as anything he could remember his father driving before. He looked at his father leaning with his hip against the fender, smiling while his buddies maligned his trade.

"Swapped him a good Ford for a old Dodge," the bearded man said.

"Hey, listen now," Mark's father replied, "I druther drive a Dodge than push a Ford."

"How bad did you get took?" the bearded man asked.

"I'm lucky I still got my britches."

Mark heard the play in the men's voices then, and he knew that the Dodge was as good a vehicle as could be hoped for. After a while his father lowered the hood, though he and the two men stood talking still. The day had gotten hotter and Mark had begun to eye the men's water jugs, though he felt too shy to ask for a drink. He felt torn between wanting to get back in the pickup so he could be cool again in the air conditioning—maybe go get a drink somewhere—between that and staying where he was and watching the big machines run and listening to his father talk with his buddies.

"They's been a few let go that was hired on after me," his father was saying.

"You ain't got no worries," the older man was saying.

"I reckon it's another six months of work with everybody kept on," Mark's father said. The way he said it seemed almost a question.

"It might be a little layoff when they quit this field," the older man said. "But they'll start up again somewheres. Birchfield's a big outfit."

"Of course, it's good money in them factories," Mark's father said. "That General Motors plant we both worked at, I made a little over what I'm getting here."

"I've done my time in them factories," the older man said. "Two years on the line at General Motors in Detroit, two at Bethlehem Steel in Pittsburgh, five at Frigidaire in Dayton. Driving ten or fifteen hours every other weekend to be at home for a day. And the hell if I'd raise my kids in such places."

"Amen to that," Mark's father said.

"It's enough of that kind of life."

"Well, I hope," Mark's father said. "I hope."

"You ain't got no worries," the older man said. "It might be a little layoff when they quit this field, is all."

---

For a moment after pulling into the parking lot of the grocery, Mark's father sat quietly. Once or twice he looked over at Mark as if he might speak, though each time he didn't. As they walked into the store, Mark lingered for a moment by the row of vending machines at the main entrance. The pictured cans of pop, all shown dripping with moisture and little flecks of ice, made him feel the dryness of his throat even more. He would have asked for some change then, but his father had already gone into the store.

It took them a long while going back and forth across the aisles to search out all the items on the list. At first his father paused before each shelf, comparing the brand names of the items to the WIC coupons. Several people said hello to him in passing, and each time he jerked his hand back from whatever he was reaching for, like someone starting from a snake.

After a while he began grabbing whichever brand of powdered milk or dry oats or potted meat or soup he came to first, stuffing the item under his arm and hurrying to the next aisle as if he was afraid of being caught at some misdeed.

At the checkout counter he handed the entire booklet of WIC vouchers to the cashier. While they were waiting to be checked out, a tall, stout woman came to stand in line behind them. Mark recognized her as one of his mother's sewing customers. He knew that she was the wife of a man who made money buying and selling land and leasing timber and mineral rights. And he remembered his mother saying how much she dreaded her because of the hard patterns and material she always brought and because of how picky she was about fit. The woman smiled at them and said "Why, hello" in a loud, cheerful voice.

Mark's father nodded to her and mumbled hello in reply, then turned shyly away. He stood with his hands in his pockets while the cashier scanned the groceries and peeled off the coupons. Several of the items she set aside without scanning, and before ringing the total she leaned close to Mark's father, holding the booklet of vouchers so that he could see. "You've got to get these brand names," she said in a soft voice.

His father stared at the few items for a moment—a box of corn flakes, a loaf of white bread, half-a-dozen packages of lunch meat. He glanced at Mark. Then he said to the cashier, "We don't need them."

As they passed the vending machines on the way out, Mark felt again how thirsty he was. He spoke quickly this time. "Daddy, I want a pop."

At first his father seemed not to hear him. And when he said it again, louder, his father leaned down to him and said in almost a whisper, "I don't have any change now. You can wait until you get home."

Mark looked down at the pavement, feeling bad in a way that he was not sure of. For a while he studied a puddle of oil and water that with the sun striking it showed bright streaks of color, and then he heard someone say something. When he looked up he saw his mother's sewing customer holding her hand out to him. "Here," she said. "Here you go."

Mark looked back at his father, but he was looking away now. He felt again the dryness of his mouth and throat. Then he took the change she offered and dropped it into the slot on the nearest machine.

The drink was peach flavored and so sweet and cold that the first sip made his teeth ache. He had not taken a second drink when his father called for him to come on, they were leaving.

As they passed their garden going home, Mark's father pulled the pickup off onto the roadside and shut off the ignition. He sat quiet again for a while, his face held stiff in a way that made Mark want to keep still as well. After a while he turned to Mark and said, "Don't you never act that way again." He got out of the pickup then and went down the path into the garden, yelling and waving his arms. Mark slid across the bench seat and looked out the door on his father's side and saw the boys on the far creek bank. It was three of the Gipson boys.

At first they hunkered down in the brush, but as Mark's father came nearer they straightened and began to kick among the weeds as if they were hunting for something along the creek bank—crawdads or water snakes. Each carried a paper grocery sack hugged close to his side. The sacks were rolled down at the top and bulged slightly with whatever the boys had gathered. When his father yelled at them, they didn't answer or even look in his direction, and when he came midway of the garden, where the cornstalks were highest, they all turned and waded slowly across the creek. By the time Mark's father reached the bank, they had climbed up the hillside and become hidden in the tangle of brush and young trees.

His father stood in the middle of the garden for a while, staring at the hillside where they'd gone. After a while he went to one of the apple trees that bordered the garden. He unfurled a burlap sack from the pile he kept there and began filling it with fallen apples. Then he began picking from the trees. When the sack was filled out, he pulled a few cabbage heads and placed those inside. He knotted the sack then and took it and laid it on the creek bank near where the boys had been standing.

Mark stayed by the pickup and watched his father walk across the garden in the direction of the house, his hands in his pockets, his head down-turned and shoulders hunched. The way he walked was like somebody carrying something on his back—a sack full of sweet potatoes, a bushel basket of corn, something heavy and awkward to handle.

Mark's father paused at the front steps of the house; he looked back over his shoulder, and after a moment he turned and started back toward the road. He walked purposefully at first, but after a few paces he slowed, and finally he stopped again. He stood with his hands in his pockets, looking from the house to the garden to the roadside, where Mark stood next to the pickup.

Mark wondered if his father was waiting for him to do something, to start carrying in the groceries or maybe even to drive the pickup to the house. Maybe he was going to let Mark drive the pickup on to the house the way he'd let him drive the old Ford sometimes when they had something heavy to transport to or from the garden.

He looked at his half-empty bottle of pop. He'd not let loose of the bottle nor taken another sip since his father had said what he'd said. When a yellow jacket lit on the mouth of the bottle, Mark tried to shake it off, but the more he disturbed it the deeper it moved into the bottle neck. Watching the bee, he thought about the woman who had bought him the pop. He thought about the salesman at the car lot and his father's buddies on the strip site where he worked. For some reason he thought about his mother and sister at the sewing machine, the baby at their feet.

He watched the bee as it darted into the surface of the pop, as it tried to rise free then of the syrupy liquid. The sound of its frantically buzzing wings within the half-empty bottle was almost musical. It was so loud that it seemed to drown out all other sounds.

# UPHEAVAL

THE CAB OF THE TRUCK feels hot already, and already Haskell can feel the film of coal and dirt gomming his skin. Clouds of dust rise high enough to pebble his windshield, so thick the roadway edge is barely seeable. He wonders who it is driving the spray truck and why they're not doing their job.

As he passes the raw coal bins, he meets George Turner flying toward him on his road grader, the machine bouncing so high on its tires that Haskell feels a gut-clench of fear. He thinks to himself, That's too fast. He's going too fast. He touches his own brakes as if to slow George Turner's grader and battles the urge to cut his wheels toward the road edge.

A shrill ringing begins deep in Haskell's left ear, like the whir of a worn bearing. He can see George Turner's face—the beard stubble on his jawline, the thumb-smudge of coal black beside his nose. It surprises Haskell how near George looks. He braces his arms for the hit, grits his teeth as the ringing grows more worrisome. Almost before he knows it then, and with no more a calamity of dust and motion than a hard wind might have caused, the grader is by and gone, not even near to tagging him, not really. The ringing in Haskell's left ear fades, becomes a little pinprick of sound near the hinge of his jaw, so slight he can almost ignore it.

Lord have mercy, he tells himself. His headache has begun to throb more strongly, and he feels a weakness in his hands, as if he's gone too long without eating. He pops two aspirin and swigs from his water jug. It had been a solid chunk of ice when he'd taken it from his freezer that morning, but the ice is melted away now, the water almost warm. I'm as nervous as a cat, he tells himself. He drinks deeply, chasing the bitter taste of aspirin, letting the water fill and calm his stomach.

If I just get through this day, he tells himself. If I just get through this day. He presses the water jug to his forehead, feels its surface moisture seep into his temples. He sees the spray truck then, parked at the road edge next to the Peterbilt that Albert Long drives. It is Jim Stidham's boy, the one they call Tad, standing at the rear bumper, fighting to coil up a hose. As he passes nearer, Haskell sees the Peterbilt begin to back toward the rear bumper of the spray truck. He thinks, Surely that boy's got sense enough to look around him. But Tad keeps on coiling the hose, neither moving nor looking up. Haskell thinks, Surely he can hear the backing alarm.

He tries to catch himself before he leans out the truck window and yells like a fool. He tries to tell himself that what he thinks he is about to see happen—Tad Stidham getting pinched between the truck bumpers, getting crushed, getting killed and mangled—is no more about to happen than he'd been about to collide with George Turner's grader. It's just him, him in his nervousness, looking for the worst to happen.

He leans out the truck window then and bangs the door with the flat of his hand and yells, "Ho! Look out there! Ho!" Tad Stidham startles so suddenly that he almost trips himself on the hose. For a moment he looks wildly around. He looks at the Peterbilt that has stopped backing a good ten yards away and is now pulling forward onto the haul road. He looks at Haskell going by in his big rock truck.

Haskell sees the expression of the boy's face change from startlement to anger, and he knows by that what the boy must be thinking—that Haskell's called warning has been just to scare him, has been just to make a joke of him again because he is low man on the totem.

The boy flings the hose to the ground and shouts something at Haskell. And though he can't hear the words, Haskell knows he's been cussed. He feels a touch of anger himself then. He doesn't cuss other men. He is angry still when he passes the walking dragline and turns his truck to get in line for reloading.

He watches the boom of the dragline swing out, a football field long. It is hard to think how big a piece of equipment a dragline really is, hard to see without some other smaller piece of machinery standing near for comparison.

He watches the bucket rake into the overburden. Tremors rise up through the tires and frame of his truck and up through his boot soles and legs, like all the ground beneath and around him is being upheaved. It is hypnotizing. One haul, a hundred tons. He feels his mind ease some as he waits, knowing he has a good ten minutes or more of sitting idle.

---

The morning breeze has died, and though the air has grown less humid with the noontime heat, it feels even muggier now. Most of the men sit or half-lie on the ground or on the tailgates of their pickups, as if to move even enough to eat is more an effort than it is worth. Others pace on restless legs, and some stand and kneel at intervals, seeming to find no ease in either position. Once and again a man will speak to say how hot and miserable it is. They sit quiet otherwise and sullen in a way not common to any.

Haskell sits next to Joe Calhoun on the tailgate of Joe's pickup. The old man's left hand is wrapped around from wrist to fingertips with a white handkerchief. He holds the hand away from himself as if neither to see it nor let it be seen. It bothers Haskell not knowing how he's come to harm himself—Joe the oldest man on the site, the least careless, the least likely to mistake himself around machinery.

Josh Owens and Bill Bates sit nearby, facing each other across a cable spool upended for a card table. They focus on their play with heads lowered, hardly speaking but to bid or pass or call trumps, their behavior so out of keeping with their normal foolery that Haskell feels his own humor made bleaker by their company.

Haskell wipes his shirttail into his eyes, clearing sweat and fine grit from the corners. His vision clears for a moment, then becomes hazy again. He bites his sandwich, and even that seems mucked, the bread made soggy by the steamy air, the baloney flavored less by the taste of mustard than the scent of diesel fuel on his hands. He pitches the rind of his sandwich toward the ditch line and takes a drink of water to rinse his mouth of the tainted aftertaste.

When he looks again at Joe, the old man's face, dark as it is with sun and weather burn, seems almost sickly. He is about to give over and ask Joe if he's all right, when a sudden, unexpected uproar commences among the card players. Haskell looks to see Bill Bates standing over Josh Owens, Bill flinging his cards in disgust upon their make-do table.

"That's enough," Bill is saying. "By god, that's enough of that." The sides of his neck and his ears have become suddenly blotched with red, and the skin of his face where it shows through the mask of coal dust has flushed red.

"Now, I don't mean nothing," Josh says, standing as well.

"You don't never mean nothing."

Haskell has half-risen to step between the two, when Joe Calhoun mutters something almost beneath hearing. Haskell leans toward the old man, straining to catch his words. "What?" he asks. "What is it?"

For a moment longer Joe sits completely still, his face pained and angry-looking. Suddenly then, he turns to Haskell and speaks in a strong, loud voice. "I said a man's got to watch. Watch himself and everybody around him. That's just the fact of the matter."

Joe stands and strides over to Bill and Josh. Without speaking he gathers up their cards in his good hand and walks on. After a few paces more he stops and turns, staring upward toward the job site.

Josh and Bill stand facing each other a moment more, then stalk off in different directions.

For a while then Haskell sits studying the big insulated cable running from the generator house to the dragline. He tries to think how many volts it carries. Sixty thousand? Eighty thousand? It is a firing offense for a man just to walk near that cable. He can still feel the motion of the rock truck in his legs and arms, and from time to time he reaches to the pickup's bed wall, feeling the need to brace himself against something solid. He rises and walks over to where Joe Calhoun still stands, still staring toward the job site.

"Got to be on your guard," Joe says. "All the time."

"You'd think a man could get some little break," Haskell replies. "Some little peace of mind."

The other men begin to rouse themselves then. Those who are still pacing stop and stand, staring a last few moments into the distance beyond the near ridges. On the leveled hillside above them the dragline works on, and the two payloaders work on to keep filled the outgoing coal trucks. As they start up the hill path toward their machines, the men raise their eyes to watch the boom of the dragline swing about, the huge bucket darkening the earth askance of its path. Haskell feels a slight chill at the back of his neck as the ground where they walk becomes shadowed. His head begins to throb more strongly.

—

Half-an-hour before quitting time Haskell hears it, a sound so faint as to be imagined, just barely out of kilter with the regular uproar of haulage—of backing alarms and rumbling wheels and buckets and blades and whirring auger bits—a lone, flat-sounding boom, like close-by thunder, like something near in distance, heavy and solid, coming hard to ground—followed by slow-growing quiet.

He guides his truck off the haul road, parks it on the level, then goes to stand with the crowd of men on the incline above the overturned coal truck. The boy is just being lifted from the crushed-in cab.

"Who is it?"

"That Prater boy. That Dwight."

"Got away from him, huh?"

The most of the coal load still lies within the side-turned truck bed, though spilled blocks strew the hillside from the road edge downward, marking the path of the wreck. Hydraulic fluid has begun to drip from a burst reservoir, a reddish stain forming as from a living wound within the litter of broken glass and metal and other odd rubbish.

"Is he killed?"

"I don't believe he's killed."

"He ain't killed?"

"No, he ain't killed, I don't believe."

In the half hour before the ambulance arrives, the men pace along the road edge and barely speak, each straining to hear first the oncoming siren. When the vehicle is spotted, finally, they all wave their arms and whistle and call out, guiding it to them. They step aside as the paramedics descend to the wreck but then crowd forward as the stretcher with the injured boy is hauled up. They reach, lifting, jostling, getting their hands in.

The Prater boy's teeth are gritted. His head and neck are held rigid in a brace. He must roll his eyes wildly to see about him. As he is lifted into the back of the ambulance, he raises an arm.

"He's a tough one," somebody calls out.

The rear doors of the ambulance close. Hands pat the sides of the vehicle in signal. Somebody yells, "Ho!" For a while then no one speaks. There is near silence across the job site. The dozers and rock trucks, the payloaders and road graders, all are hushed. Even the dragline has yet to be restarted.

In the dearth of machine noise, a soft roar can be heard, as of gathering wind. A bank of clouds crosses the sun, darkening and cooling. On the near ridgelines, the stands of fir and hickory, of beech and sassafras begin to sway. Before long the wind is passing among the men, a cooling wash of air scented with coming rain. Then several voices start in together.

"I seen a boy one time open a gas main with his dozer blade. Burned him and the dozer both up."

"That day Arthur Sexton and Sonny Everidge hit one another head on."

"You don't know what's like to happen."

They move about restlessly now, no longer tired out. They nudge one another with elbows, clap hands on one another's shoulders, jostling and play-horsing, a sudden wildness come upon them.

Sonny broke both his arms, his collarbone, three ribs, his ankle, and fractured his skull. They say Sexton never had a mark on him. Not a bruise.

"You got to watch yourself."

"Old boy I worked with at Delphi told how a deer came leaping off a highwall."

Their talk carries loudly into the stillness, their voices echoing strangely in and about the cutbanks and spill dumps and coal bins.

"Who was it to blame? That Everidge boy and that Sexton?"

"Watch yourself and everything around you."

"Crushed in the cab of a man's pickup."

Joe Calhoun stands holding the wrist of his injured hand, staring into his bandaged palm as if to answer for himself some puzzlement. From time to time he looks up and shakes his head and laughs aloud.

"It's just something that happened, is all."

"You got to watch. All the time."

"I don't remember if he was supposed to been in it or not."

One by one then they hush, their high-sounding laughter falling still, their unruly moods dampening. Finally they all stand quiet again in consideration of the wreckage. They stand as if praying, as if thinking together a single thought.

Bill Bates and Josh Owens are first to quit the assembly. They head off together down the hill path. But for Bill's height and Josh's width, they could pass one for the other, their clothes covered from cap to boot toe with grease and oil, their faces and hands blacked with coal dust. They walk near side by side, conversing in friendly-seeming terms.

The second shift comes on, and slowly the work noises start up again. As he leaves the job site with the other men, Haskell feels his own daylong pall of nervousness and worry begin to fade, his mood uplifted by passing talk of knife brands, of heat and dust, of the weekend's planned fishing.

—

Dory is there when he comes through the back door into the kitchen, where she always is when he comes in of an evening, still wearing the red Food Town smock that is the first and last garment he sees her in each day. She reaches to take the thermos and dinner bucket without speaking, without looking at him even.

He feels the calmness of the day's end begin to go out of him. He feels in its place a spark of anger coming on, over what he can't name. I've not been home five minutes, he wants to say. Not even in the door, hardly. Not even got my shoes off, hardly. But he gets no chance to speak.

The boy starts in, the way he always does, his talk a breathless gabble of noise out of which confusion Haskell hears plainly no more than "Dad. Hey, Dad. Dad." Haskell stares Dory down, his look as purposeful as he can make it. Can you do something? Now? Can you?

She tilts her head back, shaking it slowly, rolling her eyes toward the far wall as she reaches for Robbie.

Haskell passes through the kitchen with the boy still clamoring after him. He pauses just long enough in the hallway to watch Dory kneel before Robbie, to watch her place her hands on his shoulders and speak to him in a stern, almost-harsh manner that still yet settles the boy enough to hush him.

Before he goes on he notices the small bandage on her thumb. It is worn and dirty, as if it has been there for days. He notices too the dark streaks of grime on her smock, the spots of grease, the blue pricing ink staining her fingers. A bobby pin has fallen loose so that her hair on one side hangs lankly across her face. Her shoulders slump in a way that is not tiredness only, and it occurs to him that she would have gotten home hardly before he did.

He blinks and shakes his head as if to rid himself of some unseemly spectacle, of some bad odor or vexatious thought. He'd like to tell her how bad his legs hurt, how bad his back hurts. He'd like to tell her what a day he's had. I've not been home five minutes, he'd like to say.

He drops his clothes in a pile on the bathroom floor and runs water into the tub until it is hot almost to steaming. Chill bumps rise upon his shoulders as he settles himself in. He feels the sting of bug bites on his legs, of cuts and scrapes on his hands and arms, and sunburn on his neck. When the water begins to cool, he drains it off and runs more in, keeping the bath as hot as he can stand it. I don't see what she's got to complain about, he thinks.

---

The space where the oil filter fits, beside the water pump and the A/C condenser, is so close Haskell can barely get a hand in to grip the wrench handle. Then too the filter is on so tight hand strength alone will not break it loose. He will need to get leverage with his arms, his back, and there is scant room to maneuver.

He can feel Robbie crowding in at his elbow, see his shadow across the motor. Each time Haskell moves it seems he bumps into the boy. He has to watch Robbie from the corner of his eye, try to see that he doesn't cause himself harm. He's said to him, how many times, in the kindest, most patient way he knows how. "Robbie, son, there's so many ways to get hurt around a car engine. So many ways to get hurt working with tools."

But the boy is mindful of nothing Haskell tells him. He crowds in, his hands fiddling without cease—upon a hose coupling, a cable, a belt. He pulls tools from the box—pliers, a magnetic screwdriver—turning them over and over in his hands, all the while chattering about twenty-eleven different things—some animal he has seen, some cartoon show, some wrong done him by his buddies at school.

Haskell can feel the anger rising in his chest, the adrenaline surging into his arms, his hands. Just one good, hard jerk, he thinks. One good, hard pull, and it'll break loose. The loop of the oil filter wrench squeezes so tightly that the filter's soft metal casing begins to crimp, though the thread does not give. He wants to pull the wrench off and fling it into the creek. He wants to take a hammer to the filter, to the whole damn motor. Break the shittin' thing to pieces.

From the corner of his eye he sees Robbie playing with a socket wrench, ratcheting it over and over. It is a battle to keep from yelling at the boy. He takes a deep breath, then another, and after a moment he is able to cease his effort. He lets go the wrench handle, takes the cup of coffee he'd left cooling on the car fender and steps off a little ways.

When he's had his breather and his sip of coffee and is calm again, he says to Robbie, "You ever see such a tight sumbuck?"

In the moment after his father speaks to him, Robbie becomes quiet and still. He gives a hesitant grin and shakes his head.

"We'll get her," Haskell says. He props a foot upon the bumper this time, leaning further in, rocking down upon the wrench. The filter's casing crimps even more, like a beer can being crushed, but the wrench does move, or at least Haskell thinks it does. He rises on the bumper, bearing down with as much pressure and might as he can muster. Of a sudden the wrench slips loose, and Haskell heads off balance into the motor. He throws his left hand up to catch himself, bangs it hard against something sharp—a bolt, a lip of metal.

It comes out of him then. He strikes the oil wrench against the filter, against the generator, the head cover, the breather lid, flailing with it as he pushes himself upright. He throws the wrench hard to the ground, holding his skinned knuckles to the side. As the first surge of pain runs through him he curses, feeling sorry for it even at the time, but spewing forth nonetheless.

"Goddamnit," he says to Robbie, "Goddamnit, I said to leave them tools alone."

He is several minutes getting calm enough to pick up the oil filter wrench and return to his task. "It's always something," he says to himself. "Can't do the least thing without it being something, always something." He takes another breath before he speaks to Robbie. "Try not to get in my way," he says, his voice as level as he can make it. "Just try not to get in my way, is all."

He leans over the motor, fits the loop of the wrench onto the filter again. He gives a pull, and this time the filter moves. He pulls the wrench as far as the tight space will allow, getting a half turn before coming up against the generator. He slips the wrench off, replaces it, pulls. The filter turns easily now. In less than a minute Haskell has it free. "We got her," he says. He holds up the filter, dripping oil from the open end, spattering it almost gleefully, like a drunk man spilling his cup. "We got her, Robbie."

But the boy is not there anymore. Haskell walks around the car and then the yard, calling the boy's name. He is nowhere, as far as Haskell can tell, within sight or hearing. Haskell is about to go into the house and look for the boy there when he glimpses Robbie's face at the edge of the living room window just before the curtain falls to.

When he's emptied the thick oil from the old filter into a plastic jug, Haskell finds his nine-sixteenth box-end wrench, gets down on his back, and scoots beneath the car to reach the oil pan. As he loosens the plug, he tells himself that it's better anyway for the boy not to be fooling around the car while he's working on it. He tells himself there's so many ways to get hurt around a car engine. So many ways to come to harm.

---

They all sit quiet through their supper together, Dory hardly raising her eyes from her plate except to glance toward the window or the wall clock. Robbie is quiet, though Haskell is half-afraid to move lest he give the boy some unintended upset. He begins to wish more and more strongly for conversation, a joke, anything to cover a little the irksome sound of forks scraping against plates, of chewing and swallowing, but there is nothing he himself can think to say.

By the time Dory rises to clear the table, Haskell has begun to feel the first mild throb of his daylong headache coming back on him. Listening to Dory clang away at the plates and bowls, it occurs to him to ask if that noise is necessary, to ask if that noise is in some way for his benefit.

"Sit down here and rest a minute," he says instead. She continues to move as if she has not heard him, and for some reason (he is not sure why) he feels it foolish to repeat himself. He feels a tug on his arm and hears vaguely the sound of Robbie's voice saying something again and again. He blinks his eyes open, though he'd not been aware even that he'd had them closed. Dory is sitting across from him at the table again, watching him.

Haskell feels a growing urge to strike something—the wall, the table. He can see himself upending the table, kicking his chair across the room. Something, anything just to make known what he thinks of the situation.

He speaks without knowing he is about to. "You'd think a man could have just a little peace of mind when he comes home of an evening," he says. "You'd think a man could look forward to a little rest in his own home."

"You can rest," she says.

"Ain't no peace of mind around this place."

Dory leans closer to Robbie until she is almost hovering over the boy, hovering as if to pull him from harm. A splotch of light from the overhead bulb reflects from the white cloth covering the table. It brings shadows to the underside of her face, deepening the creases about her mouth, her eyes. She has become years older-looking by that light—her skin blotched and unhealthy-looking, her cheeks and eyes sunk in so that the outline of bone can be seen, the sockets and hinges. Haskell watches the mechanism of her jaw as she opens her mouth to speak.

"You can rest," she says. "Nobody's stopping you from resting."

It occurs to him to ask what she means by that, but he says nothing. In his oncoming gloom he has begun to think again about

Dwight Prater wrecking his coal truck, about the sound it had made going over, about the way the boy had looked being pulled from his truck cab, him shaking so hard from shock you could hear his teeth chatter from as far up as the roadway. He thinks again of his own near mishap, what he believes was a near mishap, with George Turner's grader, and he feels again the urge to touch his hand against something solid, to steady himself against the fitful dizziness and upset he feels come upon him again, against the tiredness.

He looks at Robbie. The boy is staring at the bare tabletop, his face stiff, a flush of redness on his cheek and neck. Dory places her hand upon Robbie's shoulder, and he seems at once to calm.

Haskell rises and walks out of the kitchen. He stands on the back porch a long while, feeling the comfort of the moist night air. When he finally feels some at ease again, he turns and looks through the screen door into the kitchen. Dory and Robbie are still seated at the table, their heads close, speaking so softly together that Haskell can barely hear the sound of their voices. He thinks how he'd like to tell her about Dwight Prater wrecking his truck, about him almost colliding with George Turner's grader. He reaches his hand to the door, pauses, then walks off the porch into the dark of the yard.

---

On his first haul, Haskell watches his truck's rear end in the side mirror, lining it up with the berm as he backs toward the highwall edge. His eyes and skin feel gritty. His feet and knees and his lower back all ache as if they'd not been rested even a single night. His neck feels tight, and already there is a dull pressure in his temples that throbs with each shriek of the truck's backing alarm. He feels his shirt pocket for the aspirin tin. Then suddenly the muscles in his back and legs and arms all clench at once, and he hits his service brakes. He leans out the window and looks hard at the ground before the berm.

The truck's engine throbs through his chest, and for a moment it is as if his heartbeat rises and falls with the idle speed. He tastes diesel at the back of his throat, feels the sting of it high in his nostrils. His head swims like he is drunk. He fumbles for the seat-belt catch, and then he realizes if it was going to go it would have gone already. He sucks deep breaths. It was not the ground giving way, he'd seen. It was heat shimmers. Or it was the shadow of a cloud passing. Or it was light on his mirror.

For a while he watches Joe Calhoun working his D-9 on the adjacent hill seam, the dozer's blade cutting into the overburden, loosing boulders and small trees toward the valley floor. It seems a marvel almost, the way the huge dozer clings to the contour of the hillside, the way the tracks sidle and shift on the near-vertical incline.

He watches as Joe Calhoun goes about leveling a large beech, first ditching the ground on the downslope and then above. In a short time the tree begins to topple of its own weight, its branches catching and snapping against the still-standing timber, its roots tearing slowly free of the ground. Joe Calhoun moves the dozer to and fro, nudging with the blade in a gentle-seeming way.

Haskell has run a dozer himself. It is as familiar as any piece of machinery on the site, but he watches it now like a man seeing something he never has before. He feels strangely like he is about to see something or know something he never has, that all he has to do is sit still long enough and watch close enough and it will come to him.

But as the beech begins to skid down the hill slope, its broken limbs shining whitely in the bright sun, clods of black dirt dripping from its tangle of upturned roots, he feels again the sensation of loose soil sliding beneath his wheels. He presses his foot even harder onto the brake pedal.

From the corner of his eye he sees Ray Sturgill sitting in his truck, waiting his time to dump. Haskell wonders how long a while he's been sitting idle just watching another man work, if it's long enough for Ray to have thought something.

He lets off his service brakes and continues backing until he feels his wheels touch the berm. Then he puts the transmission into neutral, sets the park brake, and pulls the dump lever. At the same time he guns the engine. Dust rises with the clamor of falling material from his truck bed. He can feel the truck's back end jarring, and for a moment he feels dizzy again. He clenches his hands tight on the steering wheel and raises his foot above the brake pedal. But then the bed empties out and the rear end is still again, and he is not slipping off the highwall edge but sitting stable.

He lowers the bed, puts the truck in gear, and lets off the park brake. The adrenaline fades out of him as he pulls back onto the haul road. He begins to worry then that he's forgotten something important or overlooked something important he should have seen. He runs through his morning safety checks—belts, brake linings and pads, wheel cylinders, hydraulic lines. There is nothing he can think of that he's missed.

# SOMETHING TO TELL

IT WAS MOSTLY WOMEN ganged about the front doors, sitting on the concrete steps or leaning on the handrail or standing with their backs pressed against the brick exterior wall. Some held cigarettes hidden at their sides and kept a lookout over their shoulders. They took quick puffs, turning their faces toward dark corners to let out the smoke. Others seemed to make a show of their smoking. They waved lit cigarettes around as they talked, the glowing embers making trails in the gloom.

Trina looked to go in another way, but there were no other lighted entrances to be seen, no other doors not chain-locked for the night. The voices quieted a little as she approached, the talk becoming less raucous. She went up the steps without speaking to anyone or looking at anyone directly. She was almost to the door when one of the women headed her off.

"It ain't time yet," the woman said, her voice louder than it needed to be for how close she was. She wore a black, oversized T-shirt with the image of some bulked-up pro wrestler over the words *Bite This!* The wrestler on her T-shirt, Macho Man or Hulkster or some such, was stripped bare except for his yellow trunks and high-topped wrestling boots. He posed in such a way as to be thrusting forward with his hips, both hands gesturing to his bulging crotch, so that it was no misreading the printed message.

Trina nodded as she tugged on the door. It budged enough to prove it wasn't locked, then stuck tight.

"It ain't time yet," the woman said. "I'm telling you." She smiled in a way that seemed conflicted, like she wasn't sure whether to be friendly or quarrelsome. Her lit cigarette bobbed between her lips.

Trina let go of the door and moved next to a concrete pillar, pressing back against it so that she kept outside the perimeter of the entryway floodlights. The lights made a wide circle, taking in all of the steps, fifteen or twenty feet of sidewalk, and extending several feet out into the parking lot. Moths and gnats flapped against the covered globes, making a frenzy of overlarge shadows on the bright-lit pavement.

The women were most all up into their late twenties or early thirties and of a like appearance—their shapes squared by mannish clothes, their hair either pulled back in stretchers or left to hang in limp, finger-combed strands. They stood bowing their spines out and shifting their weight from foot to foot, like they had deep backaches and leg aches. Trina could see them working at Save-A-Lot, some of them, or Arby's or Wal-Mart. They probably all had kids wearing them out.

It seemed for a while like no one was about to talk again, but then a dark-complexioned woman with a broad face and coal black hair done in braids flicked away the butt of her cigarette and spoke.

"Lord, I hope the house ain't burnt down when I get home," she said. "I left the old man with his supper in the oven and it turned on. It's untelling."

"He ain't that bad, is he?"

"Why, he's no worse than all the rest, 'bout sense enough to scratch his nuts."

They all of them laughed at that comment. The one who'd made it smiled and jerked her head to flick a lank strand of hair back from her face. One or two of the other women made smart cracks then, and in a moment whatever humorousness Trina had interrupted was returned.

"I'd like to have the kind of time on my hands like some of these men," the dark-complexioned woman said. "I wouldn't be out fishing for no bass. I wouldn't be traipsing the hills after elk."

"Would you go to a bar? Get all jacked up?"

"Honky-tonk University, that's where she'd go."

"I wouldn't go to no bar. I'd go off somewhere and be alone. I wouldn't go nowhere I could be put upon."

"A man ain't no more worth than a dog," the woman in the wrestling T-shirt said. She stood with her arms crossed, peering back over her shoulder into the building's lobby. "At least a dog can be *trained* how to act." She was not that large a woman, but there was something about her that seemed to give her size. It was how she stood, her legs braced apart and her shoulders hunched. She stood like somebody getting ready to be bulled into and to bull back.

"Well now they *have* got their uses," the dark-complexioned woman said. She grinned and glanced around at the other women, but they had fallen silent, as if unsure what to make of this line of talk.

The woman in the wrestling T-shirt made a scornful sound deep in the back of her throat. "A woman's a fool that thinks she can make over a man into something fit to live with," she said. "Marriage ain't nothing but a punishment on the woman. It's a scourge is what it is."

The dark-complexioned woman didn't reply but instead began to rummage though the big quilted bag she carried. Her forehead was crinkled with concentration, as if she was searching for something she suddenly needed. After a moment, she hung the bag back on her shoulder. "Why hellfire," she said, "hang 'em all."

The woman in the wrestling T-shirt laughed then. "That's all I'm saying," she said, with no more than a little meanness in her voice.

Several of the other women started in cutting up then. When one of them got off a smart remark, another one or two would jostle against her as they laughed. They drifted near about one another, sometimes touching one another's shoulders or wrists to claim the chance to speak. They took notice of Trina enough to look her way once and again, to smile at her when something humorous was said. None pressed her to speak though.

Their cigarette smoke hung in a light haze within the circle of the floodlight. It was not so close as to cause Trina a headache. The smell was pleasant almost. Out of doors in the evening air, with the weather a little bit fall-like and it dark but for around the floodlight, it was almost an enjoyment.

—

When Dreama let off crying and began to wheeze, Trina went to wake Shondra, and found her snuck out and gone. For a second she was torn over which child to worry over most. Then the baby squirmed against her breast and she went to wake Dwight.

It was going on six months since he'd rolled the rock truck off the edge of the haul road. He was still having to sleep in the recliner, his head and neck held from moving inside a brace they called a halo. It had a metal band that was screwed into the temples of his head and connected to four rods and a harness that fit over his shoulders. She'd told him it looked like something they'd put on a crazy person in the asylum.

He hadn't thought that was funny. "Why would they put it on a crazy person?"

"I don't know," she'd said. "To keep them from banging their heads against the wall or from biting somebody. I don't know, it's just what it looks like."

She was afraid to jostle him too hard. Even if she didn't really hurt him, he might accuse her of it later. She put his recliner in its upright position and began to pat the back of his hand. He'd drunk a beer after supper and had taken a muscle relaxer, but it was no other choice than to get him awake. She got up as close to his ear as she could and began to shout. "Dwight, get up now. Dwight, get up." Finally, she'd gone and gotten an ice cube and touched it to the back of his neck.

He came awake enough for her to get him to hear. "I need you to get up," she shouted.

"What is it?" he said. "What?"

"We've got to get to Hazard," she said. "I need you to help me. You've got to come and go to Hazard with me to the emergency room and take Dreama."

"What's the damn problem?" Dwight snapped.

Trina knew he was half-asleep still and not understanding all the way what she was saying. In any case she stood back a little. He'd not ever been threatening to her, not to her or Shondra, either one. The state he was in physically, he probably couldn't have hurt her if he wanted to. It was something in his voice these past weeks though, and in his face, that had come to make her step more lightly about him.

She pulled him to his feet, and at first he stumbled like somebody drunk. It would have been a comedy—the two of them staggering around, him trying to balance with what looked like a wire cage on his head—but the sound of Dreama's breathing was too much of a worry. Trina found the car keys and Dwight's billfold and jacket and made him lean against the wall while she got his boots on him. By the time they were out the door, he had come awake enough to begin to understand the situation.

"Do we need to call—" he began.

"Can you drive?" she asked. "Or do you want to hold the baby?"

He answered by going around to the driver's side of the car. It took a minute of maneuvering for him to get behind the wheel. He had to turn his body at an angle with his knees bent and edge in backwards.

Trina kept her window rolled up as they drove, fearful of the night air. The baby had wriggled her head so that she was up high against Trina's shoulder. It was a position that caused Trina's arm to tingle, but adjusting even a little seemed not to keep Dreama as easy. The baby's skin was dry and hot. Her face, that had been beet red, was turning splotchy now.

Dwight started off fast, but when he came up too sudden on where the road crossed the creek bed, the muffler crunched down hard against a rock. Dwight cursed as if in pain and slowed way down. Trina wanted to tell him to punch it, but she wasn't for sure how much awake he was yet.

Dreama's mouth was close up to Trina's ear. Each time the baby took a breath, it made a raspy, scraping sound that caused the hair on the back of Trina's neck to stand up. She could feel the puff and draw of air on her cheek, feel the bubble of fluid where she held her hand against the baby's chest. She began to time her own breaths with Dreama's, as if to take into herself the rawness she knew the baby felt in her throat and in her lungs.

When they passed a branch road or mine access road or even where an ATV trail had been made, Trina peered out her window, looking to see in the darkness some sign of Shondra's whereabouts. She could have been somewhere in the holler still. Though just as likely she was in Hazard or Vicco. She was just as likely out running the roads in somebody's car that was drunk or on drugs. There was no use hoping she was safe.

Halfway out of the holler, they came to a curve where the road narrowed to barely the width of a single car. A set of headlights was coming around already, shining whitely on the trees and brush of the near hillside.

Dwight eased them toward what shoulder there was. The oncoming vehicle appeared, an empty coal truck heading back up the holler to be loaded. It was going faster than it should have been and seemed so close to sideswiping them that Dwight cut the wheel by reflex. They missed being tagged, but not without dropping a front wheel off the shoulder into the ditch line.

The sudden lurch started Dreama crying again. Dwight cursed. "Don't you think I don't know who that boy is," he said. "Don't you think me and him won't be having words." Trina knew they were stuck even before Dwight touched the gas pedal again. She let him go at it though. He tried to rock them out, going from reverse to drive to reverse again. After ten minutes of that, he sat with his foot on the gas pedal, just spinning the wheels. Gravel flew and weeds and grass began to scorch, but they moved not at all. Dwight sat then as if waiting for Trina to say something, as if wanting her to. Trina held herself from speaking.

After a while Dwight hauled himself out of the car. He went to the cliff face across the road and bending only at his knees managed to pick up a flat piece of shale. It took him half an hour almost to collect six or seven pieces and stack them in front of the skewed wheel.

Roberta was the name of the dark-complexioned woman with the braided hair. The woman who'd worn the T-shirt with the wrestler on it was named Bunny. Trina sat in the row behind them in the Writing I class, near but not too near. The T-shirt Bunny had on this week was ordinary-looking enough at first sight, plain white with a big *CK* on the front. You had to look close to see the *fu* and the *off* positioned around the larger letters.

Trina liked to listen to them talk. The week before it had been men. This week it was jobs. Bunny had a job with an outfit that resurfaced the county roads. She wore a hard hat and an orange vest and carried a two-way radio. She directed traffic to stop and go around the men working.

"It's me and one other girl on a crew with a dozen men. You ain't heard vulgar till you've been around a bunch of men working. The things they say to me and her they wouldn't never say to no woman if it was any other circumstances."

Roberta said no matter what it couldn't be as bad as Wal-Mart. "Wal-Mart don't have no idea of advancing their workers. What Wal-Mart wants is as many souls as they can get working twenty-nine hours a week, making $5.15 an hour. It's unreal the kind of advantage they take on their workers."

In their first class, the week before, their instructor had explained to them about setting in a story and detail and characterization and plot. He'd read a story to them and pointed out techniques used by the writer. He drew a graph on the chalkboard of what a story should look like, making *x*'s along it where certain things were supposed to happen.

Trina could tell he knew what he was talking about. The more he talked, the more enthusiastic he became. He even tried making a joke or two at the class. It was when he got to the part about *climax* in a story, that Bunny said something to make Roberta laugh out loud, and he started getting flustered. He tried explaining *denouement*, but Bunny raised her hand and asked, "Is that where you smoke a cigarette?"

Class let out early that first night.

The first thing he did the second week was to give them an assignment to go walk around, in the building or outside, and write down what impressions they came up with. Bunny and Roberta and several of the others headed straight outside for a smoke, but Trina stayed in the building to walk the halls.

He had told them not to try to have impressions but to just let them occur of themselves. She was not sure she understood what he was asking for, and after a few minutes she began to think of going home early. Dreama's fever was down, and she was getting clear of her congestion, but it bothered Trina, her daughter staying so much with Dwight's mommy. It had been that way since Dwight's wreck, since Trina had started back in working. Then Dwight's mommy had made that remark about Dreama growing up not knowing which one of them was her actual mother. That had been after Trina had signed up for classes again.

It was odd taking college classes in the same building where she'd gone to high school. When she passed the nighttime janitor squeezing out a large gray mop in the rollers of his bucket, it occurred to her that she remembered him from back when, though she couldn't recall his name, had probably never even known his name. She nodded to him, feeling the urge to say hello, but he made no show that he even saw her.

The odor of the ammonia solution in his bucket made her nose sting, increasing the headache and uneasy stomach that had begun to come over her. She began to think she should have gone outside. She could have gotten impressions from looking at the sky. If it wasn't too overcast she would have been able to see the moon rising and what stars were out. Inside was nothing but bare walls and grimy floors and ammonia smell.

Other odors came to her as she went further along the hallway —chalk dust, mildew. As she passed by the cafeteria, though the doors were closed and it was long after hours, she was sure she could smell cooked food. The image of a green bean squashed on the tile floor came into her mind, it was no telling why.

She caught something faint then, like something imagined. As she tried to make out what it was, she realized it was not one odor but a dozen maybe. It was aftershave maybe and deodorant, perfume. It was the way somebody's hair smells from tobacco smoke, from pot smoke. It was sweat and bad breath and stomach gas. What it was, was the mingled-in odors of bodies all crowded together, all those high school kids like she had been before, milling through the hallways.

Of a sudden she had a memory of her and Dwight tangled up together behind her locker door. She could remember how his breath smelled, how his mouth tasted—like cigarette smoke and spearmint gum. She could remember how the hair at the back of his neck felt where she liked to rub it, soft like feather down, like the fur on a cat's back. It was overwhelming how strong the sense of him was, coming back on her.

She tried to turn her mind some other way, but it was no use. She remembered in spite of herself. She got a pricklish sensation between her shoulder blades, like somebody brushing their fingernails lightly across her skin. She had a feeling like warm breath on the sides of her neck. The sensations were not lasting. In a moment the memory that had stimulated them wavered. She had a brief recollection of marching at graduation, so far along with Shondra already it was no hiding it even under her robe. Then all she could think of was

Dwight in his current state of injury, of Dreama's weak health, of Shondra's uncontrolled behavior.

I wish somebody would of smacked me, she thought. I wish somebody would of smacked some sense into me when it mattered. Lord, how foolish.

Her head began to pound, and she began to feel so ill at her stomach that there was nothing for it but to go outside and stand with the smokers and hope that she could come around well enough to write down her impressions about the moon coming up or what stars were out, or clouds if that's all there was.

---

Trina wanted to forbid Shondra from answering the phone. She knew who it would be, calling right after supper. It would be a shouting match though, if she tried. And then it would be Shondra sneaking out again some night, coming home again in who knew what kind of a state.

It had got to where they couldn't hardly be in the same room together. When Trina did try and talk to her, Shondra would crumple down in on herself, her whole attention paid to chewing her thumbnail or picking threads from her clothes.

"It's your own good I'm concerned with," Trina would say, or, "You've got your whole life ahead of you," or, "You're playing with fire, young lady, and you're a-going to get burnt."

Shondra would respond with rolling her eyes or with mumbling, "Uh huh, Mommy. Uh huh. All right."

Trina had become almost afraid to go into the girl's bedroom anymore. She'd not ever caught her in the act of drugging, but she'd seen her enough times when she was coming down, lying splayed across her bed with her hair stuck out ever which way and her eyes as red as if somebody had took and poured blood into them.

"What do you think you're doing to this family?" Trina would scream at her. "You're a-tearing this family apart." But her words had no more effect on the girl than they would have on a house cat. It was no understanding whatever in her face, no awareness beyond whatever kind of stupor it was she'd partied herself into.

It was worse going in and finding her snuck off somewhere. Then it was walking the floor all night, trying not to let Dwight know what was up. "You're a-scaring me to death," Trina would say, not knowing what else to say or what way to say it.

The phone stopped ringing while she was still debating with herself over the least-bad approach to take. I just wish, she spoke to herself. I only hope . . . She didn't finish the thought aloud, though her mumble would have been too low to hear even if Dwight wasn't watching the television.

She knew what it was he thought. Sometimes she just stared at the back of his head, willing him to say it, daring him to in her mind. Go ahead and say it. Go ahead and tell me how dirty the house is. Go ahead and tell me I ought not to be working, let alone going to school of a night. Go ahead and tell me how Shondra's running wild and Dreama's all the time sick. Go ahead and tell me how bad injured you are, 'cause I don't know.

He didn't know half what was going on, and even if he did he wouldn't be no more use than tits on a boar hog. She put her head down on her arms and closed her eyes, making a little space for herself that was dark and solitary. She had a sharp little pain in her shoulder where Dreama had laid her head so long going to the hospital. She bounced her legs up and down to ease their jitteriness, her chair shaking with the motion. She'd get to sleep in a while, but she wouldn't sleep sound. Her mind wouldn't let her.

—

"Have you ever had a dream that you have to think awhile after you wake up to be sure it wasn't happening?" Bunny asked. It was about the only thing she'd said since she'd arrived. The T-shirt she had on tonight read *I still miss my ex—but my aim's improving.* The way Bunny looked made the message seem almost more sad than funny. She looked like somebody sick with something. Her skin was splotchy-looking. She had big dark circles under her eyes. What hair showed from under her Cincinnati Reds ball cap was tangled as a rat's nest.

She had a lit cigarette going in one hand and she held a Winston Hard Pack and a Bic lighter in the other, like she was getting ready to shake one out to light.

"Well Lord, I have," Roberta said. "I have one dream where I'm battling to keep somebody from coming in the house on us, and I can't move. Then it's like I'm battling to wake myself up. My old man says I cuss and everything."

There were fewer of them in attendance than there had been the week earlier, though it wasn't certain whether the absent were gone for good or just skipping. There'd be a few they never saw again, them having enrolled just for the student loan money. She and Roberta and Bunny had been steady, along with a woman from Big Branch named Janice Collins, and Janice Collins's grown daughter, Sylvia.

"I dreamed I was setting up with Mommy again," Bunny said, "her moaning and coughing up and going on herself. I woke up reaching for the bedpan."

It was getting darker sooner. It was still light enough to drive in without headlights, but by class time it would be near dark. The floodlights around the front of the building had started to come on earlier. They seemed less bright somehow, as if the lengthening darkness was more of a draw on their power. Trina had begun to stand just within the edge of the light.

One woman that had not even spoken hello to anybody hovered at the outer edge of where the light reached, near enough the group to stay a member in it yet far enough out to keep from being too much a presence. Trina had noticed her just enough to know that she always wore the same A-line dress, green with a lace collar, and that she wore her hair in plaits.

"How long did you take care of your mommy?" Roberta asked.

"It was less than a year. Probably less than six months. It's been so long. I was just young. I was just twelve or thirteen about."

"Was it you all alone?" Roberta asked. "Taking care of her?"

"Yes, it was me all alone," Bunny said. She flipped her cigarette stub at the sidewalk so hard it made a snapping sound when it hit.

Some of the other women nodded. Then they all stayed silent for a while. For some reason Trina thought about Shondra when she was a little girl playing make believe that her cats were her babies, reading storybooks to them, scolding them for acting up.

One of the women said "uh huh" softly to herself, like she was listening to some familiar tale being told, though no one else had said anything aloud.

---

The first thing she thought to write about was getting saved. It was probably something like that the instructor wanted when he told them to recall a *formative* experience. It had been just a little while after Shondra was born. They'd been living with Dwight's mommy and daddy still, and it was at their church it took place.

*The Solid Rock Church of Christ was a white church located halfway up Sassafras Mountain with a steeple on it,* she wrote. *It is called Solid Rock because of it being built out of cut stone. I had on a white robe that my mommy sewed for me. She tried to teach me sewing but I didn't have the interest and then she died a year ago.* She paused to study her sentences, tracing her pen back over what she'd written, darkening and thickening the letters. She wondered if she ought to put in how the creek was so low they'd had to dip water over her face when they leaned her back. She'd heard later how some of the old people said that wasn't full immersion, like it didn't count.

*It is a blessed day and I could feel the Lord's spirit in me and in all my family and in my brothers and sisters in Christ that are my family in the church, not my real family.*

She paused to trace over her letters again. Some of them on Dwight's side hadn't wanted her to have membership in their church, period. Some of them had downed her all the while she was pregnant with Shondra. Had put the blame on her. All on the woman. It didn't matter the man had done the same sin.

*I know the blessing of the Lord has come in me,* she wrote, *because*

*I feel light on the inside in my heart and that is the feeling of all my sins being washed clean and being born again in the Lord's eyes.*

There were just no words to describe it. Because it was being emptied out of what was hateful in you and filled back up with love. God's love, that was everywhere, and if a person would just open up your heart to Him, He would work His will in you. God was always trying to bring a person to Him, but a person has to open their hearts.

It was like her getting pregnant with Shondra when she was sixteen. It was God working His will in her. It was His way of bringing her to Him. Shondra was a blessing. She was a gift, even if it had been outside of marriage that she was conceived. The act itself was sinful, but what come of the act was innocent. What come of the act was a beautiful, innocent child.

*It was the middle of the night,* she wrote, *on the seventh of February and there had just been a cold rain that had froze on the road. I wasn't due for two more weeks but I guess Shondra was impatient to see her Mommy and Daddy and she would pick the most inconvenient time.*

That night they drove to the hospital, it was just her and Dwight. His mommy and daddy hadn't come because of the roads being so bad. Her mommy hadn't been able to come because of nobody willing to risk driving her at night on ice. Trina knew that if her daddy had been living he'd have gotten her there. She couldn't blame people for the roads being bad, she knew. Still and all.

For a few more minutes she sat and stared at the writing tablet. Then she stood up from the kitchen table and walked over to the couch. Dwight was sound asleep in his recliner. His head seemed to be floating, held as it was in the apparatus of the brace. One of his sisters had called to tell her about him wrecking. "He's killed," she kept saying. "He's killed. Oh Lord, he's killed. What will we do, he's killed."

That had been the illest feeling Trina had ever had. The scaredest feeling. She kept calm though. She didn't lose it. She just stood holding the phone, not trying to think, but thoughts coming anyway, what-all she'd have to do, what-all she'd have to know. There'd be death benefits through his job for a while, and she might have to sign up on welfare for a while. She'd get back on at Pic-N-Pay, working the register.

If she got six more hours of college credit she could substitute-teach. She'd have to do that somehow. She'd have to keep money coming in somehow and keep on with her program in school both, and keep the kids cared for.

Dwight wasn't killed. He was broke into several pieces though—one vertebra in his neck and another up high in his back, five of his ribs, his collarbone, his tailbone. He had a concussion and a lacerated scalp that took thirty-seven stitches. For a few days she'd been too relieved to realize that the weight of her situation was not much lessened by him being just bad injured instead of dead.

Dwight's working buddies had took a twisted-up piece of metal from the wreck and mounted it on a wood plaque like it was a trophy and brought it to him. Dwight had kept it on the table by his bed all while he was in the hospital. He wanted to show it off to people. He was proud. It would take a man to be proud of something like that.

She went back to the table and the notebook. She tried only for a minute to take up where she'd quit. She wrote, *In God's eyes all children are precious.* Then she scratched that out. On the next clean page in the book she wrote the word FORMATIVE in block letters as a heading. She spent a few minutes darkening the letters. She added an exclamation point. She made underlines. She put parentheses around the word. Finally she crossed the whole mess out with a series of scrawled circles and on the center of the page wrote *Tits on a boar hog!*

---

Bunny was not there the next week. Roberta said she thought that Bunny's man had come back on her, that Bunny had been saying he might be going to.

"And she's going to let him?" Janice Collins, the woman from

Big Branch, asked. "The way she talked he was the sorriest thing on earth."

Roberta shrugged. "I don't know all the details."

"She talked awful bad about him," Janice Collins said.

"I don't know all the details," Roberta said again.

For a while it went on like that, Janice Collins nosing for information and Roberta making like she didn't know any more than the rest of them. You could tell that Janice Collins didn't know how pushy she was being, how agitated she was making Roberta feel. She wanted to know, was all. Trina did too; it surprised her how much. She wanted to know what was going on in Bunny's mind to make her want to take back up with a man who according to her own words was a shiftless no-account. Did Bunny love the man? If she did, why did she? If she didn't, what else was it going on?

Janice Collins finally gave up after a while, but by then it was time to go back inside. Trina stayed outside awhile after the others were gone, her and the woman in the A-line skirt and plaited hair. They didn't speak or look at each other. They stayed to opposite sides of the lighted area, each one partly in the dark, just stood waiting.

Driving home that night, Trina was passed by a pickup truck. It came up on her and went around her so fast that she was almost startled into veering off the road. It was a light truck that had been modified to ride lower to the ground, and there'd been something done to make the engine sound louder. The license-plate holder was lit up, and lights showed around the undercarriage from bumper to tailgate so that a purplish glow flowed along on the pavement beneath.

She didn't see the driver, and she got only a quick look at the passenger. She saw that it was a girl, was all, maybe with blond hair and glasses. It was not a definite recognition, but it was enough to get Trina's mind churning, to think it might be Shondra.

The truck swerved as it crossed back into its right lane, the back end fishtailing. Trina gripped her own steering wheel more tightly and touched her foot to the brake, her stomach heaving just as if it was her going out of control. For a moment the truck seemed to get right again, but then it swerved wildly once more and glided off the road, the front bumper catching the guardrail, the impact causing the back wheels to leave the ground. The headlights flashed blindingly back upon Trina as the vehicle spun about.

She slowed as she passed the wreck, thinking for a moment to stop right there. Then she thought better and drove on until she came to a road shoulder wide enough for her to pull off. She was shaking so bad she had to make herself think how to unlatch her seat belt. It was a struggle getting the door open then and getting out. She had to lean against the car for a moment getting steady.

The truck still sat where it had gone off the road. It had spun the right way around, though only a single headlight shone toward her now. Trina had pulled off the road intending to run back down the highway. She went very slowly now, and she was only a few feet from her car when she heard the truck's engine restart.

It was even louder with whatever damage had been done. When it pulled back onto the road and accelerated past her, she could hear a clacking sound coming from the engine. The undercarriage lights had gone off, though pieces of metal now dragged along the blacktop, making a trail of bluish sparks.

The girl in the passenger seat stared out at Trina as the truck went by. She was not wearing glasses now and her eyes were as large as dinner plates. It was not Shondra—just some other girl that resembled her.

---

They were waiting up when Shondra came in the door at two in the morning. Dwight was the first to speak. He had been pacing the floor. He could bend his knees all right when he walked, but he had to keep his back rigid so that his neck contraption stayed on balance. When he turned, he had to turn his whole body, and when the front door opened he turned too suddenly and had to reach for the wall to keep from teetering. His hand slapped against the Sheetrock so hard it was like he'd punched it. "Just what in the hell do you think you're about?" he shouted.

Shondra didn't respond at first. She didn't have the mindless expression on her face she got when she was all the way gone, but she didn't look that sober either. More than anything she looked confused.

"Shondra," Trina said, "you come home, finally."

"Get in the house," Dwight shouted. "Now." He had moved to where he was almost blocking the door, his face red with agitation.

"Dwight," Trina said, "Dwight, sit down in your chair."

"I don't think I'm about nothing," Shondra said.

"Shondra, come in the house. Dwight, sit down in your chair." Trina spoke slowly, trying to keep the fretfulness out of her voice. Her trying to sound calm helped make her calm, and it would take her being calm to make Dwight and Shondra ease down.

"Dwight, sit down," she kept repeating. "Shondra, come in the house." After a few minutes the two of them stopped yelling at each other long enough to hear her. Trina said once more for Dwight to sit down and Shondra to come in the house. For a few moments longer they both just stood looking off, Dwight at the ceiling and Shondra at her feet. Then they both did what she'd told them.

For a minute Trina felt like she'd accomplished something. Then she tried to think what next to say. Shondra had come inside the house, but she still stood near the door.

"What's got everybody so much agitated?" Shondra asked. "Do you-all think I've done something? I've not done a thing."

"Oh, you've not?" Dwight replied.

"Dwight," Trina said. He sat with his hands on his chair arms, his legs stretched before him and crossed at the ankles. It was a calmlike position, though there were indentations in the upholstery beneath his fingers. He was grimacing, and the brace on his head looked more like something made to torture than to heal.

"We were just worried, is all," Trina said. "You're so late coming home, is all."

"It ain't all," Dwight said.

Trina waved her arm to hush him. What she wanted was to get Shondra just to come and sit down. She wanted for Shondra to sit on the couch by her and for Dwight to sit still in his chair. It was the most important thing in the world for that to happen. If Shondra slipped out the door on them, it would be the end of her, Trina knew it.

"We don't aim to jump on you," Trina said. "Your daddy's neck is hurting him. Why don't you shut the door before the bugs get in."

"I might go on to bed," she said.

"Don't you push it," Dwight said. "Don't you push it. You're that close." He held up his hand to show a space between his thumb and forefinger.

"That close to what?" Shondra asked.

"That close," Dwight said, holding up his thumb and forefinger again.

Shondra didn't reply. She pressed her fists against her legs, her arms straight, her shoulders dropped down like she was trying to keep a grip on something heavy in each hand. She began to chew her bottom lip. She chewed on her lip like it was a habit, like she wasn't aware she was doing it. The lip was in bad enough condition that the skin had begun to peel and split open.

"Hell, let her go," Dwight said. "If that's what she wants, let her go. She thinks she can go it on her own, let her find out. She'll find out."

"Dwight," Trina said, "just be quiet. That's all that's required of you."

Dwight made a disgusted face. Trina stared at him, trying to make her point. He raised his hand to touch one of the pins that held the halo to his skull. There were six in all. The two that could be seen were situated just in front of his hairline, above each temple. The skin around the pins was red-looking. It was puckered as if trying to grow up around the intruding metal. Trina thought about the splinter of coal her father had got in his hand one time. It had been too deep for him to pick out, and when the skin healed, it healed over and around the coal splinter, making it part of his body.

"I believe it's getting more chilly these nights," Trina said. "Shondra, close that door, honey."

Shondra put her hand on the door, though the way she stood, there was still no telling which side of it she intended to be on when it closed. Trina didn't know what to say or what not to say. She no more knew what was passing in her daughter's mind than she would have an absolute stranger's. That's what it was like, like one night her Shondra had snuck out and an absolute stranger had snuck back in.

"I've been thinking about making a peanut-butter cake," Trina said. It was the only thought she had that seemed unlikely to provoke. She looked at Dwight, knowing not to expect help but hoping anyway.

Dwight seemed to be getting over his agitation. More than that, he seemed about to give out. He had slumped down in his chair as much as the brace would allow him. The halo had come to seem so much a part of his body, Trina had trouble thinking of him without it. Dwight never said how much of an ordeal it was to wear. He said the vest itched him over his shoulders was all. She'd not thought that much about it. It was like a cast, was all, like on your leg or arm, something to protect the bones while they mended.

"I believe that's what I'll do then," Trina said.

The yellow-colored porch light showed inside enough to outline Shondra's left side where she stood half-turned. The porch light's glow made that side of Shondra's face look discolored, not yellow so much as just not natural, not healthy. Her eyes looked affected somehow too. They were not red or swollen or glazed-looking. They just didn't appear right. They didn't appear focused on what they were aimed at.

"If that's what everybody wants," Trina said, "I'll make a peanut-butter cake."

Looking at Dwight, looking at his face, at his hands clenched on the chair arms, she could see the entire misery he was in. Rising up, sitting down, walking—it was constraint without letup, every move you made, every common little task.

Neither Dwight nor Shondra was speaking now. They seemed not to be in the room even. Looking from one to the other, Trina couldn't have said which one was furthest distant.

—

It was on the TV news about Bunny's house trailer burning down. It was a big enough story for them to go on location and show the destruction. The concrete-block underpinning still stood, but the sheets of aluminum that had made the trailer walls were buckled down into what had been the trailer's interior and furnishings. The wreckage smoldered and dripped water at the same time. The yard all around was both scorched and muddy. There was a big poplar tree with its leaves wilted on the side that had faced the fire.

Bunny's name was given as Bonita Rae Newberry, said to be known to friends and family as "Bonny." She was reported as being the only victim found. The state police were said to be investigating the fire as a possible arson. No information was given as to the identity of the possible arsonist. Bunny, Trina thought. She had a feeling like somebody had took and punched her in the stomach. That's Bunny, I know it.

The teacher didn't say anything that next week about Bunny, though she seemed about all anybody was talking about outside of class. He maybe acted a little more nervous than usual, but he kept the class going. When he gave their writing assignments back, Trina's first thought was that he had wrote more on them than they had. He said their stories all had promise, but that they need work still.

What he said on her paper specifically was that although she'd depicted several compelling episodes she hadn't shown a unifying theme, an idea that tied the different events together in a meaningful way. He said for her to work on her mechanics and grammar and gave her a C plus for a grade.

What he talked to them about that week was what he called the universal conflicts, which was Man versus Nature, Man versus Man, Man versus Society, Man versus Machine, Man versus Self, and Man versus God. The question that jumped up in Trina's mind was, What about man versus woman? That's what Bunny would have said. She looked at Roberta when she thought it.

It seemed like a small number that stood outside for break. Roberta told as much as she knew, or said she did. What everybody thought in Bunny's family was that her man was the cause of the trailer burning. Which is what everybody had told the state police.

He had a record as long as your arm and had spent as much time in jail as out. His last conviction had been for dealing prescription drugs. He might not have been in trouble for a while, but that didn't fool anybody. It didn't fool Bunny, though it was her that defended him, her that kept him up despite all, that ran him off time and again, then each time turned around and took him back.

From the expression on Roberta's face you couldn't have told what she was thinking or feeling. Her face was just stony-looking. Her voice sounded like somebody making an announcement on the loudspeaker at Wal-Mart. She went back inside before she'd even smoked her second cigarette.

Nobody else seemed eager to speak right away. There were not even lightning bugs or moths fluttering or the sound of frogs peeping to break the stillness.

She wondered whether she should ask what other people made on their papers, whether it was correct or not to do so. She wanted like anything for somebody to start talking. She wanted like anything to stave off the glum thoughts she'd be having if she wasn't distracted.

What she did, trying not to think about Bunny and about Dwight and about Shondra and about everything else, was to compel herself to do so all that much more. She thought about Bunny's T-shirts with the raunchy sayings on them. She thought about the puckered-looking skin around the screws of Dwight's halo. She thought about the sound Dreama made trying to breathe. She thought about what she'd been able to make herself not think about since the night before—Dwight and Shondra spitting poison at one another. She thought about the face of the young girl in that truck she'd seen go off the road. She thought about being told by Dwight's sister that he was killed.

The quiet made her feel like she was having her guts wrenched out. It made her feel like she was being beat with something. It was nothing for it but to say something, she knew, say something or have her head split open.

Trina moved in closer amongst the other women, near enough to touch shoulders or hands. It was not an uncomfortable nearness. It was not like standing near to people she barely knew. She made to speak, then stopped.

At the far edge of the group, the woman in the A-line dress and plaid overshirt was moving in out of the dimness. Her grayish-blond hair hung in a long plait over her shoulder, and she kept her hands busy fidgeting with the tufted end. She glanced around briefly, then looked above all their heads. You could see by her expression she had something to tell. The women moved a little closer together within the radius of the floodlight, almost like people warming themselves at a fire.

# DONE AND FINISHED

SHE JUST TOOK OFF walking, not even a coat on, not even her head covered up. It was like she couldn't walk fast enough. Shondra's legs and even her arms and hands trembled with needing to move, her heart beating so fast it seemed like to lurch from her chest. The hell with them, she thought; the hell with them, the hell with them. She made fists and swung wildly, left after right after left, making the rainfall spatter, getting satisfaction from that slight violence. The hell, she thought and swung, with them.

The road dipped her sideways. Shondra didn't realize falling—just found herself sprawled and flailing in a mud hole, not able to get standing again. It would come to her later, the apprehension of herself lying splayed in the middle of the road in the dark where the coal trucks ran. The thought would bear upon her, and she'd have to fight it from her mind. She'd have to argue with herself that she hadn't done anybody wrong. Hadn't killed anybody. Hadn't stole. Hadn't broken any commandments she could think of.

She kept conscious owing to the cold, it soaking through the seat of her jeans, running a shiver from her muddy rump to the back of her neck, that least bit of soberness enough to get her moving toward standing. She crawled on knees and hands along the hardened ridges of tire ruts until she got a sense of level ground, then reeled to her feet. "Shit fire," she said. She doubled over and retched, her head aswirl with sparking lights. She lost awareness for a moment, stumbling, yet somehow not falling again. "Shit fire."

If she looked straight up, Shondra found, looked straight up into the rain so it ran down over her face like somebody pouring it from a pitcher, she could keep from seeing the light sparks and swirls and black dots in front of her eyes. She was desperate not to pitch over again. Her face, her whole head—scalp and neck and ears—felt hot, like with a fever. Her dizziness too was like a fever. The suffering on her insides was like being sick with poison. "I ain't got nothing to say for myself," she said, the rainfall sputtering off her lips. "What is it I'm supposed to say?"

She stood like that an unknown amount of time until finally she came clearheaded enough to know better where she was and how she'd come to be there. It had been trying to *avoid* the big uproar that she'd made Chase even bring her home. And where had that got her? Shondra could remember something getting broke against the wall, and her the one that threw it. They both had been screaming though. Her and her mother both had been screaming.

The only light to see by was what came from people's houses, the porch lights and front-room lights. It was not enough to go by and not fall in a hole. The temptation dogged her though—dark or not, rain or not—to keep right on and see couldn't she get back to Chase's house. She could line the journey out in her mind to where it seemed like something doable. Down out of the holler walking and along the four-lane toward Perry. Ride to Hazard with somebody. On to the mouth of Quicksand. Up Quicksand to Three Mile.

For a while she stood trying to decide to do it. She'd just have to walk a ways, was all. She'd be back over there. It was just walking out of the holler. She took a step that was neither forward nor back. Go on if you're going, she said to herself. She was shivering cold though, and when her teeth began to chatter, the need of getting warm became most present in her mind.

There was nothing for it but to turn about, to track the house lights back up the holler until she got somewhere she could be.

---

Shondra came somewhat awake to raised voices. Her mother's ragged and shrill-sounding, like when she was on the edge of crying. "I wash my hands of her." Her grandmother Mag's hoarse, as deep almost as a man's. "Don't say that now."

She could not open her eyes at first for the light, so bright and painful that even when she covered her face with her arms, she could not block all the harshness of it. She dared not even try to raise her head or move her body. She was ill-feeling enough keeping still.

"I mean ever word. I'm done and finished." It was her mother's voice again.

Shondra slit her eyes open just barely. Above where she lay, she could see only a blur of hanging garments. She opened her eyes more until she could see that the room was crammed full of clothing. Pants, shirts, coats, even a few suit jackets hung on hooks around the walls. In one corner sat an abdominal exercise machine, the rails and handlebars lined with a selection of unmatched skirts and tops. She shut her eyes then, having located herself. It was her grandmother's house she had made for, not her mother's.

What she needed now was to get back asleep. She'd been dreaming before, and she tried to remember what. She drifted and it came upon her again. It had been people sticking pins in her, people stabbing her with knives, people holding her down to bite and to scratch her. She fought to come more awake. Not none of it, she told herself.

"I wash my hands of her."

She began to think of Chase, wanting to will herself into a dream of him. Chase on his guitar. On his guitar, with no shirt on and a cigarette wedged underneath the strings at the peg head. *Peg head* is what he called it. She made a fantasy of putting her hand on his bare shoulder, feeling down the nubs of his backbone, underneath the waistband of his jeans. And him playing. The music chords passing through into his body from where he held the guitar against him. The music like it was coming through from inside him, making a quiver against her hand.

Shondra drifted off on the comfort of this imagining and even slept a brief time in peace before the bad people came back upon her with their sharp claws and stickpins.

The light from the window had gentled enough not to blind her eyes when she opened them again. Her head ached terribly when she rose up though, and she felt other hurts when she went to stand. Both her arms felt strained and sore-muscled. Her left knee, her hip, her right shoulder—all felt maltreated. She had to walk limping, steadying herself along on whatever she could reach—the footboard of the bed, the dresser, the door facing.

The hallway outside the bedroom lacked nearly any light, and that was a mercy. Shondra went by feel along the narrow track between stacks of cardboard boxes and overstuffed paper and plastic bags. When she reached the dining room, she covered her eyes with the back of her arm and grasped for where she knew the light switch to be.

"Is it up from its sick bed?"

Shondra wouldn't have known her grandmother Mag was in the room but for her speaking and for the cigarette smoke. The woman sat at the dining room table amid heaps of clothes and kitchen utensils, old books, cassette and vhs tapes, appliances, board games and puzzles, electronics, children's toys, two or three VCRs.

Shondra had to shift a box of kitchenware—mismatched dishes and cooking pots jumbled in with all assortment of forks and knives—to clear a chair for herself at the table. Her grandmother held her cigarette in the corner of her mouth, her head tilted so the smoke drifted away from her eyes. She was printing numbers and dollar and cent signs on self-adhesive labels and sticking them to whichever toaster or clothes iron or pan without a lid that came within her grasp.

"Let me have a cigarette, Mag," Shondra said.

Mag touched a finger to the soft pack that lay open on the table, and Shondra reached to snake one out. She thought to ask what time it was, but then she heard her mother's voice, as if she was right there speaking. What time is it? Are you for sure you know what day it is? What month it is? Do you know what's the year? Do you know your own name even?

Mag had had her hair done just recently, styled straight and cut just above shoulder length and with highlights put in. She went to pains to keep herself up. It was talked about in the family what pains she went to.

People ought to care how they look—that quick the argument leaped into Shondra's mind, her mother's imagined voice so grating it made her teeth hurt—ought to care what's thought of them.

It's my own business how I look like.

Like a tramp. Like somebody that don't care nothing for herself.

It's nobody else's concern.

Like some old ragpicker.

You're a one to talk.

And then the crying. It was all designed at her, Shondra knew. Her mother going to bed with a headache. Poor suffering thing. Look how pitiful. Oh, look how I'm done. Shondra almost let herself speak, she was so mad of a sudden. Mag, it comes to the looks department, you win out over me or Mommy, either one.

Yeah, that's some contest.

There was no remark Shondra could think of that didn't sound like smarting off, none that she couldn't already hear the sarcastic response to. It was best to keep quiet anyway, as much as she could, until she knew better what ground she stood on, what side Mag was coming down on.

Her grandmother finished her cigarette. She didn't speak but to ask for her lighter. Shondra passed the lighter, and her grandmother shook herself out a fresh cigarette. She shook one out for Shondra to have ready.

They sat smoking for a good while in the half dark and clutter. They two were like people on break time from some job. Here in a little while they'd have to get back to it, but for now they could take pleasure just in not having to move.

---

That first day all that was expected of Shondra was to clean the bathroom and vacuum the hallway and living room and dust the furniture a little. She went slow so as not to make her head swim and took breaks to lie down or have a smoke or watch TV. Mag kept close watch, but as long as Shondra didn't make for the front door or the knife drawer in the kitchen, the situation kept calm.

If the phone rang and Shondra was in the room, Mag would pull the phone back into the hallway as far as the cord would reach, or else she'd stand with her back turned and speak low, her hand held up to cover both her mouth and the receiver.

Shondra wanted to wave her arms and yell, "I ain't crazy. I ain't on drugs."

Mag was uneasy too, Shondra knew. If she wasn't sorting her bagfuls of goods, she was searching through cabinet drawers for something she needed suddenly or rummaging in the back corners of the pantry for some odd object, or else she was climbing on chairs to swipe at cobwebs nobody but her could see, or she was switching through the TV channels, or she was coming behind Shondra to do over her dusting.

And then there were the coal trucks that went tearing by every five minutes. The road was in ten feet of the house, and the trucks were so fast-going and so heavy and jarring that the windows in the house would shake and the dishes would rattle in the cupboard. Each time one passed, it felt to Shondra like an iron spike being driven through her head. It caused her teeth to rattle and her hands to tremble. It caused a vibration right in her nerves, it seemed like.

When three or four oversized loads went by at once, she covered up her ears and screamed, "I'm about to jump out of my skin!"

Her grandmother didn't have to say anything to that. Shondra knew by the look on her face.

She started to say, "I ain't crazy and I ain't on drugs," but she had enough mind to catch herself. She managed to keep on with her chores, though the more she worked, the more angry she became. They think I'm easy told what to do. They think I'm easy controlled.

She upset the globes on a row of three kerosene lanterns when she went to dust the mantel behind them. She caught and set them all aright before they could fall, but it was a struggle not to pitch globes and lanterns all against the hearthstone of the fireplace.

What she did was throw the damp rag she'd been using across the room. "This is stupid," she said, louder than she'd meant to.

Her grandmother Mag sat at the dining room table, returned to the task of price-tagging her rubbish. She showed no sign that she'd heard Shondra's blowup, except that the cigarette she held in her mouth went unlit and she kept making to write a price tag with the cap still on her marker.

Shondra thought to say something about the situation, but the sight of her grandmother trying so hard not to admit any unsettlement kept her from speaking more. Speak, she wanted to tell Mag; go ahead and say it. She thought to pick up the cleaning rag she'd thrown down, but even that seemed like an uncertain action. The only clear course was to go back into the spare room and shut the door and stay there hidden.

---

This last time she and Chase had driven Chase's truck up to Cincinnati and stayed the night with his cousin Shelby. Where Shelby lived at was in a motel room he rented by the week. It was nearby the interstate, and when it got nighttime they'd brought chairs out and sat on the edge of the parking lot where they could overlook the interstate and drink beer.

At night the lights of the cars coming and going over the bridge to Cincinnati had begun to streak and blur together. Shondra had let her eyes go out of focus until it became like watching water run, like watching a stream of water, a water-flow of headlights—running down out of the mountains and down into the flat country and the big cities, up into Ohio, toward Indiana, toward Illinois, toward whatever it was there and beyond.

They didn't go in until it got way late, and then Shelby took out a big briefcase, like a lawyer might carry, with a combination lock in the lid. He'd opened it to get them out some weed to smoke on, and she'd glimpsed a few baggies of different sizes and bottles of pills and some loose cash and a big pistol. That night when she was stoned and half-gone asleep, she'd been roused by the sound of the motel room's door opening and closing, and she'd looked to see Chase bringing in the black plastic garbage bag that had rode behind the seat of the truck. He'd given the bag to Shelby. Shelby had opened it and looked in and took a deep breath of what was inside.

She'd known what was going on, and she thought, What the hell. It made her feel like something. Like it was something big going on, and her a party to it. Chase had let her drive coming home. She'd gripped so tight to the steering wheel in the traffic between Cincinnati and Florence that her hands and her arms all up into her shoulders had been sore. She'd felt like she was a different person, felt like it until the roads began to narrow and the hills to rise and grow close around, until everything began to look like what she knew again.

The bed was still unmade from where she'd lain recovering the day before. It seemed like the boxes and bags of clutter had accumulated since she'd last been in the room. She had hardly a body's width of bed to lie on. There was no way she could turn and not have some mound of secondhand clothing or cast-off junk be pressed upon her. It was like being swallowed up in a waste heap of other people's belongings.

In amongst the loose piles of unsorted clothes was a cardboard box containing all sorts of paperback books, outdated magazines, even a few old encyclopedia volumes. Most worthless of all was a milk crate filled with record albums. The albums had been stood on edge and left to lean upon one another inside the crate, and the stack as a whole was becoming misshapen under its own weight.

She trailed her hand over the edge of the bed, reaching beneath the skirt and up under the box springs. She found the rounded corner of the cardboard box and above it the splintery plane of a bed slat. She felt along the slat until she came to the hole she'd gouged in the mattress batting. Stuck inside the hole, she found the little velvet bag Chase had given her. The bag was purple with the design of a crown on it in gold and in gold letters the name of the whiskey that had come in it. It had a gold-colored drawstring.

Inside the bag, rolled in cellophane, were the scant leavings of a marijuana bud, still on its stem. There was a package of rolling papers and a hemostat she'd bought at the flea market. There was a little clump of foil with half a Xanax inside. There was the guitar pick Chase had given her. There was the Zippo lighter with Dale Earnhardt's name written like a signature and with the number of the car that he'd been killed in, number 3. The number 3 had angel wings on it. Chase said the lighter was a collector's item.

She clicked the lighter's lid open and thumbed the wheel. It rolled stiffly against what flint remained. The flint sparked, but there was not fluid enough to flame. She took the half a Xanax and lay on her side for a while, clicking the lid of the Dale Earnhardt lighter open and shut. She thought how if somebody looked in the room they might take *her* for a pile of rags, of fabric remnants or some other odd clutter. She dozed off finally, despite the sense of being too cold and of smothering.

Shondra's mother kept away another two days. Mag had been having long sessions on the phone with her, four and five times a day, thirty and forty minutes at a time. The side of the conversation Shondra heard had Mag speaking sternly against whatever demand it was being put to her. It tickled Shondra, her mother being mothered, being scolded, like it was her the misbehaver of the family.

"No, I don't believe I would," Mag would say, or, "It's no use thinking like that." What gave Shondra the most satisfaction was Mag losing her patience and calling Shondra's mother foolish. "Foolish; that's foolish. It'd take a fool to believe that."

By the time Shondra's mother did come, Mag was so far aggravated that Shondra had the hope her grandmother might come to side with her just for spite. What Mag did was sit on the couch like a stone statue.

Shondra's mother kept quiet as well. She sat leaned forward on the seat cushion of Mag's rocking recliner, like any minute she would get up and leave. She stared at the floor, the look on her face like she was about to cry, now and again making that throat-clearing sound that went all over Shondra.

Shondra knew how that game worked. What her mother wanted was for Shondra to become irritated enough that she made some sarcastic remark or said a curse word. What she wanted was the motive to pitch a fit, to get them both worked up and raving and then her break down and start crying and make Shondra feel the cause of it.

Shondra's main impulse was to just get up and go. Just get up and go. If she had a car she would. She'd get in her car and fling gravel all the way out of the holler. She had to make herself sit there and not speak. It was nerve-wracking, her mother's throat clearing, the ticking of Mag's birdsong clock, every five minutes a coal truck.

Shondra knew what she wanted to say, what she ought to say. You think you can keep control of me, she wanted to say. You better think again. You'll be awful bad fooled. She was close to it. Ooohh, she was close to it. Go ahead and say it, she told herself. It's what she needs to hear. Go ahead and say it. But then her mother did speak.

"There's some things . . . ," her mother said and paused, still looking at the floor. "There's certain things . . ." She paused again for a longer time, frowning, like she no longer had in mind what she'd been going to say. She was ill-looking, but it was how she wanted to look, that baggy overshirt clutched around her like somebody freezing to death, her hair hanging down limp over her face. It was all for effect, her acting like she didn't have the will to speak, like she didn't barely have strength enough in her body to keep sitting upright.

Shondra rolled her eyes. She couldn't help it. She rolled her eyes and let her head loll back to show her annoyance. She glanced at her grandmother, hoping to trade looks with Mag over her mother's play-acting. Mag was not responding though. She had no more expression to her face than somebody asleep or dead or knocked out. She didn't look like she was breathing hardly. She just sat stone-still, watching Shondra's mother, waiting for her to speak again.

"It tears my heart," Shondra's mother said. This time when she paused she seemed to choke up.

Here it is, Shondra thought. Here we go. She knew what words were coming now: It tears my heart, you out doing what you're doing. You're not fooling anybody. You're not fooling a soul. The only one you're fooling is yourself. Don't you have no respect? For yourself? For your family? Don't you realize? Don't you even realize?

Her mother didn't say any of it though. She didn't start in crying, which was the next antic Shondra would have expected. She didn't sigh or give Shondra a blameful look. She did take a handkerchief out of her dress pocket to blow her nose and wipe her eyes, but she was no more showy about it than if she'd been caring for a head cold.

She stood up and swiped her hands down over her legs. She did it a couple more times then, the front and back of both her hands. She combed her fingers back through her hair, which took some of the shadow off her face and some of the sickliness.

"I may as well go to the house," she said.

Mag got up too. It was *her* face that had the upset in it now. Her that looked close to weeping. Shondra's mother put her hand out, and Mag clasped it in both of hers. It was a gesture like people made between themselves at funerals or in hospitals. All that remained to be said was bless you, though neither of them said it.

"Shondra," Mag said and gestured at her. "Shondra." But her mother had gone out the door already, besides which Shondra had no idea what she could have been expected to say.

---

One jar was turquoise colored, the other a sort of pinkish orange. Shondra had spotted them behind a cardboard box on the shelf below the canned tomatoes when she went to the cellar to smoke her little scrap of dope. The box was so badly moldered that when she tried to move it the bottom stuck to the shelf and a jumble of metal screws, bolts, washers, nuts, and insulated wire upended loudly onto the cellar floor.

She had cleaned up the mess at once and then replaced the box so as to make it look as undisturbed as possible. When she thought about it later, the worry she felt at so trifling a mishap seemed foolish. It was all just so much rusted-together junk, of no worldly good to anybody. And yet she had returned to the cellar twice that same day to check for any stray bolts or washers she might have missed and to readjust the box's position on the shelf.

It was the kind of thing she had caught herself doing more and more of the last few days. She would fret over whether she'd weighted the lid of the garbage bin against stray dogs, whether she'd left out food enough for the cats, whether she'd left the light on in the pump house when she went to put rock salt in the water-softener tank. She might rise from bed of a nighttime to check whether or not she'd locked the front door and closed the picture-window curtain in the living room.

She asked her grandmother about the jars on a day they were sitting on the front porch breaking beans. They were fall beans, the hulls thick and speckled with yellow. How old were the jars, she wanted to know, where had they come from, were they worth anything. Mag didn't answer, didn't even let on at once that she'd heard Shondra speak.

Shondra didn't mind Mag not answering right away. She had found her grandmother's Percocet prescription finally, hid in an old coffee can in amongst a stash of fast-food condiment packets—ketchup, mustard, mayonnaise, Percocet. When Mag placed her hand on Shondra's arm, Shondra smiled, it was such a pleasant sensation. "It used to be common for people to send their children to stay with somebody," Mag said. "With a grandparent or an aunt or somebody. I almost was raised by my grandmother."

The weather that had been turning the fall cold so early had shifted out. There was sun on the porch. Yellow jackets drifted in the warmth, seeking amongst the bean pods and about the foil pie plate used to feed the cats and about the mouth of the soda can they'd set out to tamp their cigarette butts into.

"She got her heat by burning coal in the grate of her fireplace,"

Mag said. "She had a pine floor that the resin would ooze up out of, it got so hot around that grate. The wind would gust down the chimney and blow soot in the warm resin."

Mag was quiet again for a space. She stared off intently, her fingers working steadily, snapping off hull ends and pulling strings in so quick and regular a motion it was almost hypnotizing to watch. Shondra could not keep pace with her grandmother, her fingers so fumbly that the beans went into the bowl raggedly broken or with strings and hull ends not all pulled away.

"She'd have me up in the middle of the night scrubbing soot," Mag said. "When it was good weather she'd heat water on the stove to scrub the porch with. That yard too. She used to take a broom, now, and sweep it. Sweep it till there wouldn't be a track in it, not a sign."

"Sweep the yard?" Shondra asked.

"I'm telling you."

Shondra could feel the touch of her grandmother's hand on her arm still. Her hand had been cool-feeling and dry. She had the impulse to touch her grandmother's arm in the same way, to grasp her hands even and warm them and rub away the bluish patches that lay beneath the skin. She didn't though.

The same night she'd found Mag's Percocet, she'd managed a call to Chase. She didn't risk talking long to him. They'd whispered awhile to each other.

Mag dusted the scraps of bean hulls and strings from her lap and reached for another handful to break. Shondra spent awhile dusting herself clean as well. A confusion of strings and hull ends had grown between them on the porch glider. They looked so knotted together in their mattedness, it was untelling where one ended and the other began. They seemed to make something—a bird's nest, a snarl of fishing line—what exactly Shondra couldn't tell.

---

That Saturday early, they loaded Mag's quarter-ton pickup with the goods she'd tagged. They loaded with no order in mind, boxes on top of bags on top of whichever loose objects came first to hand, fragile or not. When the space was wedged as full as the pickup's camper top would allow, they forced in a pair of folding card tables and two collapsible camp chairs. Neither the truck's tailgate nor the camper top's lift-door would close. Mag ended up weaving a cargo net from an old clothesline that she secured with half-a-dozen double knots to the truck's bumper, the tailgate hinges, and whatever other odd lip or flange of metal she could find to serve for a tie-down.

Mag drove, the bench seat adjusted as far forward as it would go to put her in reach of the clutch. When they passed her mother and father's house, Shondra caught herself crouching down in the seat. She sat straight upright at once, though for some reason that response seemed no different. Done and finished, my ass, she muttered to herself. It tears my heart. Ooohh, it tears my heart.

Twice they had to steer to the road edge to make way for oncoming coal trucks, and for one quarter-mile stretch they had a Mack so close up on their bumper they could see the driver pick his nose in the rearview mirror. Shondra wanted to give him the finger, but Mag, knowing her granddaughter's mind, kept swatting her hand down. They finally came to where the road shoulder was wide enough that they could pull off. "That son-of-a-bitch," Shondra said. "I had a gun I'd shoot him."

"I don't reckon," Mag said.

"They think they own the road," Shondra said.

"Well, we got a pretty day," Mag said.

It was about a sick-looking day, is what Shondra thought. It was about a vile-looking day. It was about an evil-looking day. There were some few trees with fall color in them still, what ones had turned in the first place—a few oaks, a few maples. The leaves on most of the trees had gone brown even before summer was past and then fallen in the first cold rain. There were pine trees even that had gone brown, big patches of them on the hillsides and up on the ridges.

Done and finished. Shondra thought of how her mother's face had looked, so blank she could have been wearing a false-face. She'd looked like somebody going to a funeral, going to the hospital, enduring some such dire occasion. It was likely all a put-on, all a show.

So what about it, I go off with Chase? So what about it? It was all a big to-do over nothing. All a big stir-up. Over nothing.

In places, the ridgeline was bare of trees altogether, the timber logged or otherwise cleared for mining. In places, the ridgelines had been themselves removed and you could see through to where the machines were running, the earth movers and big trucks, gutting out the coal.

Her mother's car had been sitting with its nose aimed at the road. Shondra's father would have turned it about, so she didn't have to back out into the curve of the road and get hit by somebody driving drunk or by a coal truck going too fast. They were both of them afraid like that. Whatever bad could happen, would.

Shondra thought to say to Mag, You want to know what it's like? It's like having a prison warden over you. It's exactly what it's like, you want to know. You ought to know. You ought to realize. It's like having a jail sentence on you.

The creek running beside the road had risen and fallen the last few weeks. It was muddy, almost black. In the places where the bank had been low enough for the water to top over, there were thick leavings of mud in people's yards and garden plots, coming almost to the foundations of some of the houses and house trailers.

There'll be no coming home this next time, Shondra thought. Like a jail sentence.

Every third or fourth property had a house trailer set nearby the frame house, people's children moved in next to them. Even the graveyards were situated on the homeplaces, the markers grouped upon the hillsides with little fences around them or with steps leading to them, the dead in the family kept in almost as close a proximity as the living.

This next time, she knew it, there'll be no coming home.

Half a mile from the mouth of the holler they came to the Calvary Free Will Baptist Church. The church building sat across the creek on a little rise of land above a fenced pasture. The building was long and narrow, constructed of concrete blocks painted white. There was no steeple, just a large wooden cross affixed to the roof peak. Around the next curve and on the opposite side of the road on a graveled lot was the Church of the Nazarene. It was the newer building, looking more like somebody's home than a church. The exterior was red brick. There was a steeple, a handicap ramp, and an outdoor bulletin board for announcing sermon topics and for posting Bible passages. The God of Prophecy Pentecostal Church couldn't be seen from the road. The turnoff was marked with a hand-lettered sign, the meeting house itself situated almost a mile up the branch road.

And then they were turning onto the four-lane. Thank God, Shondra thought, though really there was no raising of her mood. She watched for the mile-marker signs and direction and distance signs, knowing by heart when each was due to appear—30 miles to Hazard, 65 miles to Jackson. Mag made no attempt at conversation. Shondra was grateful for that. She was relieved to keep her face turned toward her window, to keep hidden that she'd begun weeping. It was no wonder people drunk and smoked and took pills, she thought. It was that or go to church.

The flea market was located on one end of the big, leveled-off lot just before the Hazard turnoff. The lot was the tip end of the big strip-mine site that extended through two counties. The larger portion of the ground had been improved enough to support a Super Wal-Mart, an RV dealership, a Hardee's restaurant, a bank, and a liquor store.

Where the flea market was set up was not blacktopped or even graveled yet. The ground was as it had been left—rocky and haphazardly sloped, still scored with the track and tire patterns of earth-moving machinery and beginning to be run through with crags from water drainage.

Mag parked next to a man selling out of the back of his truck. He had half-a-dozen bushel baskets filled with sweet potatoes and apples and a few big cushaws and pumpkins to show. On a plywood board laid across two sawhorses, he'd set out pint jars of honey and grape and berry jelly, along with quart jars of beets and pickled corn and sauerkraut.

"We got a pretty day for it," Mag said to him.

"If it don't come another rain," he replied.

It took Mag and Shondra working together to unknot Mag's make-do cargo net. Shondra helped unload the boxes and set up the card tables and camp chairs, but she was not allowed to help sort or arrange the actual items. Mag had a certain order in her mind, a pattern of what went next to what according to type or use or condition. After a few minutes she had became so busy making her display that she had no notion of Shondra slipping off.

It was deception in a way, Shondra knew, but not like it was planned. She had not known Chase would be at the flea market, just that he did go there oftentimes, him and his buddies, to look at shotguns and hunting rifles. She had not determined to meet him, not until she saw his pickup parked off to itself at the back edge of the lot. She didn't go directly to Chase but made a path in and among the tables and the little fruit and vegetable stands and the parked cars and trucks and vans that people were selling out of. In just a minute she was clear of Mag's seeing.

Shondra didn't hurry even then, though. What she did was keep wandering amongst the sellers, as if she had no other intent in mind. When she stopped at a table she would look to see that Mag was not coming behind her, though she knew she was free to herself now. She could go and be with Chase, and nobody could have a thing to say about it.

There were all description of wares to be found. One man had a table that was all old tools—handsaws and rusted hoe blades and ax heads and other odd-looking objects she had no idea the purpose of. He was whittling a hoe handle from a long, slender piece of whitish wood. There were other, similar handles leaned against his table, short and long, all smooth-surfaced and tapered so as to fit specific tool blades.

Shondra couldn't figure why anyone would want to buy a handmade hoe handle, or for that matter, a hoe so wore out it needed its handle replaced. There was Wal-Mart no more than fifty feet away with every known item in the world, every tool a person could want, she would think, hoe blades and handles already attached.

She paused for a while to look over a table covered mostly in trinkets—bracelets, bead necklaces, bottle-cap openers, earrings, refrigerator magnets, novelty thimbles, and spoons. Dispersed amidst the table's clutter also were a dozen ceramic figurines of farm animals and cats and dogs, some having the purpose of saltshakers or creamers or gravy bowls.

Here's competition for Mag, she thought, junk on top of junk. She looked toward where Mag would be, wondering if the old woman had even noticed her missing yet. She could probably slip back still, if she wanted, slip back and be gone again.

At another table a man and woman, both so overweight they were breathing heavy just sitting still, were selling crafts—cornshuck dolls, hand-quilted purses and American flags, throw pillows shaped like hearts or snowmen or patterned with flowers or chickens; wood carvings of animals and laminated pieces of wood with different sayings etched into them—Jesus is Lord, Gone Fishin', such as that.

Propped in the center of the table was an oblong-shaped wall clock fashioned from a crosscut section of wood. The wood was laminated and had wide-spaced growth rings that looked more imitation than real. The hands were set at the very center of the cross section, the wood there redder and darker and softer-looking.

---

When she saw Chase, his back was to her, not even the side of his face visible. She knew his form, though, as well as she knew what eye color he had. She didn't call out but went quietly up behind him, slipping her arms around his waist, her thumbs into the belt loops of his jeans. "Hah," she said, jerking his hips back, sticking the point of her chin into his shoulder blade to make him flinch.

"Hey now," he said, twisting about and putting his arm around her shoulders. He smiled at her and pulled her snug up against him. She kept one arm about his waist as they started walking, her thumb still hooked through a belt loop.

She tried talking as they walked, about her being held almost a prisoner the last week, about her mother being such a bitch—trying to manipulate, was all. About her and Mag breaking beans one day and about today coming to the flea market, hoping she'd see him but not expecting, and then there he was. There his truck was.

It was too awkward-going, though, the ground being so uneven and Chase's legs being so much longer. Shondra kept falling out of step and then had to skip or jog to catch back up. She couldn't keep her breath to talk like she wanted to.

The boy Chase had been talking to tagged along after them. Shondra didn't recognize him as one of Chase's cousins or buddies, as anybody they usually partied with. When they came to Chase's truck, he got in the cab with them, and Shondra had to scoot over until she was almost in Chase's lap so as not to touch legs with the boy.

Chase didn't look like he thought anything of it. He didn't say anything when Shondra whispered, "Can't we get shut of him?" He didn't tell the boy to get gone or come along, either one.

The boy had a smell to him, either in his clothes or from himself, that was like ammonia, and he couldn't keep his hands still. It was like he had a condition. His hands and fingers moved like he had no control of them, no awareness even—touching his cap, pulling at the brads of his denim jacket, his fingers fumbling together as if to work some object, lacing together to make senseless gestures and signs.

"Chase," Shondra whispered, "Chase." But all Chase did was to lay his arm around Shondra's shoulders, not like he was hugging her so much as getting himself better situated. They sat there another minute at least, neither Chase nor the boy nor Shondra saying a thing. The boy chewed on his thumbnail for a while and then began to pick at a sore on his chin.

Finally Chase made a gesture with his hand and said, "Break it out."

What the boy broke out was a little paper sack from the inside pocket of his denim jacket. From the sack he pulled a butane lighter and a little cellophane baggie with its corner tied off to hold several chunks of what looked like the rock salt Mag used in her water-softener tank. It wasn't rock salt though. Shondra knew what it was. The last thing the boy took out was a broken light bulb with the screw tip missing. He dropped one of the crystal chunks into the bowl made of the broken light bulb and sparked the lighter beneath it.

—

It started raining. Big drops, far between at first, struck and stuck whole to the pickup's streaky windshield. In just a minute the spatter became a soaking rain, so heavy as to diminish all seeing beyond the truck's cab, so loud as to drown any possible sound otherwise, whether speaking or laughing or songs on the radio.

What came over Shondra was close to the best feeling she had ever had, so good she almost moaned when it came over her, the pleasure occurring in spasms—through her thighs, through her hips and belly, through everywhere. She still held the light-bulb bowl, its heated glass suddenly like a piece of burning coal in her hand, that increased sensation also wonderful.

We sat and broke beans one whole day, she said, or thought she said. She couldn't hear herself. And smoked cigarettes. Mag smokes worse than I do. She smokes like a chimney. I swear, them damn coal trucks.

It was nothing like smoking pot. She felt like she wanted to get out and dance or run. She smiled over at the boy Chase had let come in the truck with them. Rain was spitting in from around his door. He was getting out and leaving. That's all right, Shondra said, or thought. Going out into the rain seemed the most likely thing in the world for somebody to do.

Mommy said she was giving up on me, Shondra spoke again, or thought. Said she was washing her hands of me, said that actual thing.

She began to laugh. The nonsense of it. Every bit of it. "Chase," she said, "Chase." She heard herself speak aloud. Then music exploded throughout the truck, some guitar player who Chase worshipped, a frantic run of chords thrumming from the speakers behind the seat and in the doors.

Shondra laughed. Chase was intent. He was like a kid, his hands moving wildly, making chord positions, strumming, his mouth twisting as he mimicked the violent playing.

Shondra cackled. She doubled over laughing, tears coming from her eyes, her sides aching, even her face beginning to hurt with how wild she was letting go. "Oh, God," she said. "Chase. Chase." He was laughing too, eyes closed, head thrown back, his hands flailing as the music reached its max, keeping on even after the song came to its sudden finish, the both of them laughing and laughing.

In a while their fit eased, their rapturousness dimming to where they felt overalert, was all, and crazily well-pleased. The rain had slackened too, the sun reappearing somewhat, making a prism to appear on the truck's windshield. "Oh, my God," Shondra said.

"Let's go somewheres," Chase said. He started the truck and they lurched forward, tires spinning on the newly slick ground.

The prism disappeared. Shondra leaned her head to see up through the curving windshield. A bank of storm clouds still half-hid the sun but were passing off, the sunlight breaking through in unreal-looking shafts. It was like a religious picture. All it needed was Jesus ascending, or angels, or God peeking through from Heaven.

"Let's go to Alaska," Shondra said.

"Mexico," Chase replied.

They drove around the back of the flea market. The rain had come in fast enough that most people had not had the chance to pack up. Most had just waited it out and were emerging now from their cars and from under their tarps. Everything had been soaked, junk and treasure alike, every whirligig and dream catcher, every old bicycle, every hand-carved walking stick and candy dish shaped like a rooster.

"San Francisco," Shondra said.

Everything had a sheen to it—car hoods and windshields, water puddles and power lines, people's eyeglasses. Everything plastic, metal, or glass made a sparkle as the sun shone upon it. Shondra saw the clock and sign man patting his items dry with a towel. She saw the tool man, sitting in his chair as if he had never moved. She couldn't spot Mag though. She saw Mag's truck and her card tables and goods, but not Mag.

She kept looking back as they entered into the super center parking lot, the huge red letters of the Wal-Mart sign gleaming above them.

"I ain't going to no San Francisco," Chase said.

She watched for Mag as long as she could, until they pulled onto the four-lane and turned toward Hazard. What last she saw, or thought she saw, from the vicinity of Mag's setup was a sharp wink of brightness, of color.

# THE TIMBER DEAL

DWIGHT HAS BEEN NEEDING to stand to get his back in a different position for twenty minutes now. It feels like somebody jabbing the point of a needle into the back of his neck, the pain shooting from his head down deep into his hips. What he needs is to get his neck into the traction harness for a while. Or else he needs to stretch out, have his wife pull on his legs until he's less jammed up. If he could just stand and lean on the table for a while. They'll all look at him, though, if he gets up and starts hobbling around. He hunches his shoulders a little, trying to get his spine to arch. What he needs is for everybody to be gone. He's just not been able to get down to it, what needs to be said and discussed.

Trina sits holding Dreama. Their daughter is shy of so much company. She is listless-seeming too, as if she might be getting another fever. Dwight has made them all listen to her chest at one time or another. He swears he can hear a sound, like a gurgle or like a hiss, like the sound an inner tube would make leaking air, like a valve that's sputtering. He can hear it, he'll say; whatever these doctors say different, he can hear it. And if he can hear it and him not a doctor, what is it *wrong* with these doctors?

Russell coughs. His brother has his cap and sunglasses on, so there's no telling if it was a sound made to urge Dwight on. The smell of cigarettes is strong enough on him to give Dwight a headache. It bothers Trina, Dwight knows, the trouble they've had with Shondra, and now here Russell come in on them. He's laid down the law to Russell. Russell knows. He better know.

"Perry Central's got this boy," John James says, suddenly. "He goes to make a cut, make a dribble penetration, there ain't a player in the district can oppose him."

Dwight can no longer keep from business, he knows. He braces his hands on his knees and raises himself up in as normal a way as he can. He feels his face getting hot and wishes he'd kept his own cap on when he came inside. The circles of scar on his temples from where the brace was attached, the halo, stand out more white when he blushes. The cramped pain in his lower back eases some with the changed position, though he still would like to pace around, stretch and bend.

He has thought of no good way to begin. He wades straight in. "You know how we've been talking about the homeplace?" he says. "About the timber? About leasing the timber?" When no one replies, Dwight gestures with his hands, seeking what else to say. "How about we go ahead and do it? Lease it."

It's really only his sister Helen he's talking to. Helen and her man, that is—John James. It's them he's waiting on to reply. What Helen does is cross her legs and begin to pick at something on the knee of her slacks, a piece of lint or a thread. She spends a moment then swatting at the cuff of each leg. She glances at the face of her watch. "Mamaw and Papaw's place," she says finally. "The homeplace."

"You remember, we all talked about it before," Dwight says. "It ain't a new idea."

"I thought we'd decided against it," Helen says. "Didn't we decide against it? When we realized how much a ruin it would cause on the property?"

"I don't think it would cause a ruin exactly," John James puts in. His voice is almost hurtful in the close kitchen. Russell claims he's come to talk louder since the election. "You'd have to have a haul road made. You'd have to level off an area to set your machinery."

They're one another's match, Russell likes to say of Helen and John James. They're a pair. They deserve one another.

Helen scrunches her mouth up, like she's got a taste of something sour. She puts her hand on her stomach and turns a little bit away, as if to keep something in, her temper, her disgust at what's being said in her presence. She makes a good show of her upset.

"Do you need something to settle your stomach?" Trina asks, reaching to put her hand on Helen's knee. "Crackers and a 7UP?"

Helen waves her hand to say no. "I've always had the idea somebody might want to live back there," she continues. "One of us might want to. One of our children might want to."

Dwight is about to respond, to ask Helen what children does she mean, what children does she have. Trina heads him off with a look before he says anything.

"I remember going over there with Daddy," Helen says. "I remember we'd go and visit Mamaw and Papaw. I remember like it was yesterday." She begins to twist her wristwatch again, sliding the bracelet up her arm, making it snug, then loosening it once more. She doesn't look at any of them. Instead she watches out the kitchen window.

Trina touches Helen's arm to get her attention. When Helen does look at her, Trina doesn't say anything. She nods her head as if to question. Helen nods back, her face softening, the frown lines lessening around her eyes and mouth. She verges on smiling somewhat.

It's an odd difference that comes on her in that moment. She looks pleased, not only with herself but with Trina, who's holding her hand now, and with John James, who she gives a shy glance to. It's the most agreeable-looking Dwight's ever seen her.

I can coax her to it, he thinks. I believe I can now.

Russell pipes up then, him silent all night but for when he needs to be. "Daddy did talk about logging back there," he says.

Helen's scowl comes back at once. "Why even ask me?" she says. "Dwight and Russell have decided it all. Why even ask me?"

Dwight catches himself about to throw his hands up. He puts

them on his hips to hide the motion, pressing his thumbs into the small of his back on either side of his spine. He tries to roll his head a little, but the muscles in his neck seem not about to flex even slightly. It will do no good for him to say anything more, not now it won't.

For a while Helen and Russell stare at each other, a purposeful silence between them. Helen is finally the one to break off, though it's untelling where Russell's eyes are behind his sunglasses. Helen looks at John James, and John James says, "Well, I guess we need to be going."

Trina rises with Helen, and the two of them walk out ahead of the others. The men loiter on the porch while the two women and the little girl walk out into the yard. Trina and Helen give each other hugs. Dwight has no idea what that's about. John James smiles oddly and shakes Dwight's and Russell's hands before going down the porch steps to join his wife. "Crackers and a 7UP," Trina yells to Helen, "and you call me."

---

There's still dew on the ground when Dwight goes out in the morning. It's about the only time of day he actually feels good, his back rested well enough to attempt something like work. He argues with Trina that going to the garden is what he does for rehab, that it's just as good hoeing corn as doing waist bends and leg lifts. He no more believes what he says than she does. If he gets to the end of a full row without freezing up in a spasm, it's a little miracle.

The stalks are up past his head now, and the corn is beginning to tassel. Before long it will be full enough to draw the coons and deer. I knew what's good for me, I'd just let them have it, he thinks.

He can hardly keep bent long enough even to swing a hoe the right way. He no more than gets into a good rhythm than he has to stop and straighten up and wait out the pain warnings. And it does him no good being mad at Helen. If anything, he has to slow down and concentrate on not swinging the hoe so hard he torques his back or chops down a cornstalk.

Helen can't see past herself, is what it is. She can't see anybody's interests but her own. If John James had fractured his back in two places, it'd be a different story. If he'd broke his neck, it'd be a different story told. She'd be after leasing that timber harder than any of them.

The sun is striking the far edge of the patch by the time Dwight finishes the first row. The dew is beginning to burn off now. Vapor can be seen coming off the cornstalks, turning to a least bit of mist. Dwight has been made wet passing amongst the dripping blades. His shirtsleeves, the legs of his pants, the cap on his head—all are damp. The smell of the field too is like a vapor—dirt and cornstalks, cut weeds.

For a little while, then, that is all he has a sense of, his lone notion to raise and drop the hoe in as regular a way as he can, and for as long a while as he can. The grain of his hoe handle is raised and rough-feeling. The hoe has been left laid out in the field so often, the wood swelling or drawing tight according to the weather, warping so as to be made particular in shape and even in heft. The blade too is one of a kind, so old and worn it has almost the shape of a half-moon.

Helen doesn't know what she's saying, is all. Nobody would live back in there. Nobody could. Nobody had. In years. It's untelling how many years. How long has it been since Mamaw died? That old house. You'd have to tear it down to the foundation and build it new again. It's what their daddy had said.

The wood has warmed where Dwight grips the hoe handle. It seems to him the handle is more curved where his hands are placed, more curved as if to fit his hands. Probably, he holds it in the way his daddy had. He can feel a sore spot coming on the thumb of his right hand. He won't go long enough to make a blister though, or a callous. It's the manner of standing that will get to him, of keeping bent over even so slightly.

There ain't hardly a road back in there anymore. You can't hardly get *to* the place anymore. Helen doesn't know what she's saying, is all. *Live* back in there. You'd do well to get *to* the place. If John James hadn't drawn a paycheck in eleven months, it'd be a different story told.

Dwight pauses at the row end, looking back at his work. It's been a fair job—he's turned the dirt up around and between each stalk, shaving away the weeds on both sides, not missing any that he can tell. It's a little something accomplished, he thinks.

The satisfaction he feels doesn't last a minute. He begins his second row in a hurry, as if to beat out the sun coming across the stalks. He gets further than he should, halfway and more, before the damp is drawn fully from the air and his back begins to twinge strongly enough to send him to the house.

Trina looks poorly rested in the mornings. She looks tired out even before she leaves for her job—her face puffy, the veins showing in her eyelids and on either side of her nose. Dwight has tried to tell her it does no good worrying. Shondra gets to needing money enough, she'll call. She gets to regretting her circumstances enough, she'll call.

"Can you get Dreama's breakfast?" Trina asks. She leans over her mug of coffee as if to be wakened by the steam.

Dwight has been to Wal-Mart just the one time when Trina was working. He'd taken Dreama. That was the reason he'd settled on, Dreama wanting to see where Mommy worked. They'd made a circuit of the entire store before getting in line at Trina's register.

They were ten or fifteen minutes then, waiting out the orders being rung through before them. It was odd a little bit. Trina had on the blue Wal-Mart smock they all wore, with her name tag and yellow smiley-face sticker and American flag pin. When she started checking somebody through, she said, "Did you find everything you were looking for?" When she had them done she said, "Thank you for shopping at Wal-Mart." She did like they all did, like all the cashiers did.

When it came their time to check out, Dwight couldn't think

of what to say that didn't make him sound foolish to himself. Hello sounded foolish. So did How's it going?

"I could have brought home anything we needed," Trina said, shaking her head as she scanned the few odd items they'd picked up—a box of bandages decorated with cartoon characters, children's shampoo, a roll of paper towels, a box of snack cakes, a replacement head and gas mix for a string trimmer.

"Well," he said.

Even Dreama seemed put off by the circumstances, keeping so still that Trina reached across the counter to feel her forehead for a temperature.

For several days after then, it was like he and Trina were in dispute, going around each other not hardly saying a thing, not saying what was the matter or even that something was the matter. Dwight still couldn't say what the upset was about. It was odd, was all.

"My back's about to kill me," he says now.

Trina keeps the coffee mug held before her mouth, blowing on the steam before each sip, her eyes half-closed. She's trying to get the good from her last few minutes, trying to make last what enjoyment she has left of the morning.

Dwight is about to say again about his back when she sets her mug down, hard enough that the least bit of coffee sloshes over the rim. She gets up and stuffs a chair cushion in behind him. She gets his prescription pill bottles from the cabinet and lays out his muscle relaxer and two 500-milligram ibuprofen. She gets his half-glass of milk to down them.

"You ain't going to finish your coffee?" he calls as she leaves out the door. "Come back and finish your coffee."

---

Russell's trailer is at the far end of the garden, far enough from the house that Dwight and Trina don't have to see it every time they walk out their front door. The trailer's not quite the eyesore it was when Russell had it hauled in. He'd taken a power washer and scoured off much of the grime. It's still to be determined whether it will stay on the place long enough to justify underpinning and to have the roof and sides repainted.

Dwight glances through the screen door to see Russell sitting on the couch. He raps on the door frame and waits with his back turned until his brother has time to put on his shirt and call him in. Russell keeps his arms covered for the sake of his tattoos. Except for the marijuana leaf and the *R P + J S*, all Russell's body art was acquired during his time in the pen.

It's what you'd expect—a string of barbwire circling the biceps of his left arm, the barbs drawn as if to puncture the skin and blood dripping, one drop for each year of time served; a pair of bird's wings fluttering above a crosshatch of bars on his left shoulder; various letters and numbers and symbols that have no meaning outside the jailhouse running all up both forearms and over his shoulders. On his right arm he has the figure of Christ on the cross framed by the words *He is Risen* and *Savior.* Nothing you wouldn't expect to see.

In a moment, Russell yells for Dwight not to keep standing outside. He is sitting hunched up, his knees pressed together, his arms drawn in as if to keep from touching somebody sitting on either side of him.

"I don't mean to bust in on you," Dwight says.

"I heard you coming in time enough to hide my liquor bottles," Russell says, "and to flush my cocaine and my Oxycontin pills. I hope you wasn't wanting to party."

"You have been sipping a few," Dwight says, nodding at the beer cans on the coffee table.

"I had some Mennonites come around earlier handing out literature," Russell says. He motions for Dwight to sit in the lounge chair next to the couch. "They're known beer drinkers." He hesitates a moment. "It's the nonalcoholic flavor," he says, handing a can to Dwight for inspection. "Foam but no fizz."

"You work today?" Dwight asks. He eases into the low chair, feeling the discomfort to his spine almost at once. There are no extra cushions in sight and he won't ask Russell for a pillow.

"I work tonight," Russell says. "I'm on the beltline." He makes the motion of gripping a pry bar, raising and jamming it downward. "I'm picking slate."

"That hurts me to think about it," Dwight says.

"It hurts me actually to do it," Russell says.

Dwight nods, and for a minute neither of them says anything else. They both look around the room, as if appraising the quality of the furniture or the condition of the floors and walls. But for the few cans on the coffee table and the full ashtray, the main room is fairly neat. There are no unwashed clothes strewn around or dirty dishes or much of any clutter really. Russell's work boots and three pairs of athletic shoes have been left on the floor by the front door, but they are lined up in a row together. It is a well-kept space for a man living to himself.

Russell claps his hands lightly together then. "I knowed there was something I wanted to show you," he says.

He reaches beneath the couch and begins pulling out and sifting through varied magazines—*Discover, People, Newsweek, Sports Illustrated,* not any of them the sort Dwight might have expected him to have stashed under his couch. "I get choice of whatever it is the county library is throwing out," he says.

"I see," Dwight says.

What Russell finally digs out is an issue of *Grit and Steel.* "Boy I work with gave me this," he says. "He's all into it." He flips through the magazine from back to front, then hands it to Dwight. It's open to a page advertising different breeds of fighting cocks—Grey Tormentors, Claibornes, Fardowns. In the center of the page is a bird with a rusty red head and throat, its body black with a trim of white on the back and black tail-feathers with red tips. "That's a Madigan Claret," Russell says.

Dwight studies the picture for a few minutes while Russell clears the coffee table of the nonalcoholic beer cans, emptying what contents remain at the kitchen sink, then rinsing the cans and dropping them into a paper grocery sack set next to the garbage can. He brings a damp dishrag to wipe down the table and takes the ashtray away.

"I guess I'll approach Helen again before too long," Dwight says.

He places the open magazine face up on the clean table. "I believe we just have to go at her the right way, is all," he says. "Not make her feel like she's being ganged up against. You know how she is."

Russell sits on the couch again and leans over the coffee table to read from the *Grit and Steel* ad. "Listen to what this breeder charges," he says. "Brood hens two-fifty, brood cocks five hundred."

Dwight shifts his position in the chair, leaning to one side and the other and then forward. He rises more out of agitation than pain. He walks into the kitchen area, twisting his shoulders, trying to get the cracking sound that comes with cramped vertebrae being eased.

"Pullets one-fifty," Russell continues, "stags two hundred, eggs seventy-five a dozen."

There is nothing sitting out in the kitchen, no evidence of anything that Dwight can see. Russell knows there will be no allowances made. He knows how fine a line he has to walk. Trina has not been unwelcoming, but she's made clear what limits she expects.

Helen still yet won't speak to Russell even to say hello, won't hardly be in the same room with him. Their sister's opinion when Russell got caught was, "No sympathy. He deserves what he gets. No sympathy."

When Dwight asked her what she meant by that, she got a look on her face like she'd been slapped. "What do I mean by that?" she asked.

Russell is still hunched over the cockfighting magazine when Dwight paces back into the living room. Russell is working a WWJD wristband between his fingers, twisting and stretching it around his hands in quick circles.

"I'm planning how to finance my own truck," Dwight says. "Won't nobody else hire me to drive, I'll hire myself."

Russell looks up for a moment as if seeking what to say. He nods his head and slips the WWJD band onto his left wrist. "I'm in agreement with whatever you say on the timber deal," he says.

Dwight nods. He stands in the doorway awhile, looking out. He can see the whole of his corn patch. Beyond, his and Trina's house is only barely visible, hidden by the cornstalks and by the two poplars in their yard. It will be wintertime before the sight line falls bare. "You faring all right then?" Dwight asks.

"I'm doing fine," Russell says. "Ain't a thing I need." He glances down at his hands, running a finger beneath the WWJD wristband. "I do appreciate you and Trina letting me set up over here," he says. He turns a page of his *Grit and Steel* magazine. "Daddy did talk about selling that timber over there," he adds.

As he makes to leave, Dwight glances around at the clean, clear space of Russell's dwelling place. There's not much of any feature to recognize Russell by, or anybody for that matter. It shows no more sign of being home to somebody than a motel room.

---

Dwight always waits until the sun gets low to take Dreama to the garden. If it's open enough going, he lets her walk, but through any weeds he carries her on his hip. Even if the way is clear, he likes to pick her up. It's better all around that Trina doesn't see him doing this. He can't seem to communicate that it hurts no more carrying Dreama than not.

Dreama has a toy hoe and a rake and a bucket. Dwight stands and leans on his own hoe while she digs in the play garden she's started. She plants sticks upright in the little mound of dirt and drops blades of grass and little stems and bits of straw over all.

"You're the best hand to garden ever was," he tells her. "I couldn't make do but for you helping me."

He's said to Trina, more than once, that if there's anything good come of him getting bad injured, it's the time he's had to spend with Dreama. He means it too. "I'm thankful for that much," he's said. "I've had an opportunity give to me. A person can miss out on so much in their life and not even know it."

Trina has told him, "Good for you. I'm happy for you." She's also told him, "You don't know the first thing, not the first thing. You don't even have a clue."

A few nights ago, sometime after one in the morning, the phone rang. By the time Trina got to it, there was no one there. She swore it must have been Shondra. Who else would it be at one in the morning? Who else would be calling if not her, wanting to talk, wanting to come home? Trina had stayed up until daylight waiting for her to call back and then gone unrested straight to work.

Dreama makes a square border around her garden with the small rocks she scratches up. They have to be of a like shape and color or she won't accept them, and even then she's careful about their arrangement, laying a larger rock at each corner and lining smaller ones, exactly sized and spaced, in between. When she's satisfied, the two of them go to the creek together to carry water for her crops.

When Shondra first left, Trina had said, "I hope she's got what she wanted. I hope she's satisfied. Because I'm through worrying. I'm through. I'm through with it all."

"Amen to that," Dwight had agreed.

A minnow pours from their bucketful of creek water, so small they neither one see it until it flops out among Dreama's pretend corn rows. Dreama grabs for the silver flash, scooping it up in both hands with a layer of garden dirt. The tiny fish flails desperately, its gills working, mouth gulping until it is coated in grit. "Daddy," Dreama says, "Daddy."

He can't remember a time Shondra wasn't in some kind of trouble, wasn't making grief for everybody, everybody. He'd yell himself hoarse trying to get her to listen. He'd threaten to smack her, and she'd sit there and just stare at him, just daring him to. Yes, he was relieved when she left out finally. Yes, absolutely.

The minnow flips from Dreama's grasp, and Dwight goes quickly to his knees to scoop it up again. It's a move he shouldn't have made. The first spasm freezes him solid. It's a searing, ripping agony—the clusters of nerves compressing between his vertebrae—like having a knife blade twisted through into your spine and held. He reaches for something to grasp onto and goes, "Ah! Ah! Ah!" as the pain surges, then fades enough for him to catch a breath, then surges again and fades and surges. He laughs a little, unable even to ease himself on down to the ground. "God!" he groans at the intensity of the pain. "God!"

He hadn't even known the truck was going over until he'd felt the steering wheel being yanked out of his hands. It was frightening being flung around inside the truck cab, glass bursting over him, the roof staving in, the doors staving in, dirt flying into his eyes and ears and nose. But that steering wheel being yanked out of his hands and the next instant feeling the ground tilting out from under him—that's the memory that comes back on him, not the crash or the injury trauma. Having that steering wheel yanked out of his hands by force, he wakes up reliving that.

At some point, the intervals of relief begin to outlast those of suffering. He takes a few deep breaths and chances moving. He's able to stand, deeply bent at the waist, his hands propped on his knees.

Dreama is still chasing the minnow, he sees, catching it in one hand, then dropping and catching it in the other. That's how short a while his ordeal has been. The minnow flashes sunlight in its struggle, and Dreama keeps right on it, determined beyond any thought otherwise to grasp and keep hold of the silvery flicker.

She encloses it finally in both hands and makes off for the creek, not looking to see even if he is coming behind her. He loses sight of her as she passes through into a patch of horseweeds taller than her head. He can't move yet to follow. He can call her name, is all—to tell her to stop, to not go into the creek where it's deep, to not get snakebit, to come back where he can see her.

"What do you mean by that?" Trina had asked. "'Amen.' What do you mean by that, I'd like to know?"

---

The cortisone shot has worked wonders, though Dwight is still having to keep flat on his back for long shifts. To get up and down he rolls onto his side and pushes against the mattress with his elbow, careful not to put even the least degree of strain on his lower back.

Trina has taken three days off work to tend him. "I can't expect them to give me no more," she's warned.

Russell comes by each noontime before he goes to his job. He'll stand around, swinging his arms, waiting for Trina to tell him there's nothing needs done. He tries to make conversation. But what is there to say?

"How you feeling?"

"Like shit."

"You need anything?"

"I need my back not to hurt."

Dwight can't help but get annoyed at him, at everybody really, but with Russell for some reason it's more of a struggle not to let his aggravation show. Him and his tattoos and his cockfighting magazines. Him and his wristband on his arm, like a wristband on his arm is proof against dumb-ass behavior. Because that's all the excuse can be made for where he's come to, to be blunt about it, is dumb-ass behavior. WWJD.

"You look about as useless as I feel," Dwight tells him, the third day he comes by. Even with his sunglasses on, Russell can't keep hid how the comment strikes him. For a moment then Dwight has a panicked feeling, believing certain he's about to see his thirty-year-old brother start in crying.

Russell makes a joking reply, though there's nothing much cheery in either his voice or the set of his face. "I resemble that remark," he says.

The only thing Dwight can think to say further is, "Well."

Trina gives it to him later. "Maybe I shouldn't say anything," she says. "Maybe I shouldn't speak." She stands at the foot of the bed, her hands on her hips.

"Speak," Dwight says. He catches himself patting the mattress. He wants for her to sit, to not stand in so deliberate a way as to be staring down at him.

"But it seems to me," she says, "a person in the circumstances your brother is in, the last thing he needs to be told by somebody, the *very* last thing he needs to be told by somebody is how *worthless* he is."

"I never said *worthless,*" Dwight says.

"You never said *worthless?* What did you say?"

"I said *useless.*"

"*Useless,*" she says. "Lord, God. *Useless.* Well, it's a world of difference."

"It's some difference."

Trina doesn't respond but to continue staring at him and to shake her head. Dwight knows what she means to imply. She can't believe what she's hearing is what she means to imply. He's in the wrong, he knows, but he's in the right too, just as much if not more. He can't say it. He can't explain it. In the right about what? What is he in the right about? Cockfighting, he wants to say. Russell's sitting over there reading about cockfighting. Cockfighting! Russell is just a part of it though. Russell is just a piece.

"A person has to have a value in themselves," Trina says then. She moves closer to the edge of the bed. Dwight's uncertain still whether she will sit with him, but then she smoothes and straightens a corner of the quilt, making a space for herself.

Dwight watches her, waiting for her to finish her statement. It's the time of day the sun hits the house most strongly. The box fan in the window keeps the air stirring enough that the heat is not too noticeable a discomfort. It's just how bright the room is made, the light so direct as to show every least smudge of grime—on the window glass, on the dresser mirror, on the bedside tabletop where he has been setting his drinking glasses and coffee cups. Cobwebs are showing and wall and ceiling cracks and stains from where the roof has leaked.

The light is unfavorable to Trina, making her face seem leached of color, making more of every blemish she has and every crease. "Then I don't know what," she continues. Dwight looks to see wetness on her face, wanting to see it. The motion of the blades in the box fan throws a flickering shadow, though, so that there's no telling for certain the expression of her feelings.

He knows he should be saying something to her. He should be saying it's not her at fault where Shondra is concerned. If it's anybody the failure, it's not her. If it's anybody to be blamed, it's not her. He knows he should say that to her. He knows he should reach out and put his hand on her arm and say, You done all in your power. You're not to be blamed in the least. Not in the least.

He doesn't speak though, or reach out, the dread suddenly coming on him that she might slap his hand away, that she might say to him, Well, who is it to blame?

Dwight's not certain at first that he isn't dreaming the telephone ringing. He answers it still half in his sleep, speaking as he wakes, not completely aware of what he's saying, not aware at all of who he's saying it to. He smacks the sides of his face and shakes his head, fighting the hold of his night medicine. "I'm up," he says. "What'd you say? No, no. What'd you say? I'm up."

No one speaks in reply, though he has heard a voice. He knows that much. It was not just him that had spoken. It's not a dial tone he's listening to. "What'd you say?" he asks again. Trina moves beside him in the bed, disturbed but not yet woken.

He keeps himself still, concentrating to hear. There's music coming through, muffled like at a distance or through a closed door maybe, not a tune so much as an ongoing thrumming of instruments. There are voices of people talking, also as through a door, at least one distinguishable as a man's and another a woman's. At last comes the close-up sound he's been listening for. It's no more than a sigh maybe, or just a throat-clearing sound or a cough held back, but it's right directly in his ear and it's as familiar as a voice would be. "Are you all right?" he says softly.

Dwight waits for something to be said in reply. It's coming, he knows. It's right on the verge. He knows what it will be almost, or what he wants it to be. He's anxious of saying anything himself now, of coughing, even of moving.

A prickle of heat begins on his scalp. He raises his hand slowly, scratching the places where the halo brace had been attached. The scars are more discoloration than hardened skin, but he can find each by touch. He missed the halo when it was first taken off. He'd become so well used to the weight and cumbersomeness; he'd felt unbalanced without it.

Right after Shondra left out, all Trina would do was sit by herself and cry. She wouldn't speak to say what she was feeling or to answer somebody, to say she was hungry or cold or needing to be left alone or not needing to be left alone. It had been a torment to her, chasing after Shondra, worrying after her, not knowing ever where she was going to be or where she'd been or what pills or liquor she was on or what other drugs.

Trina couldn't have taken it much longer under the circumstances. That was the truth of it. It had been a blessing when Shondra left out on her own. But for a while after it was like Trina lost all ability to function for herself, like she lost energy and willpower when she should have been feeling relieved of all that torment. She came back around gradually. In a week or two she was able again.

You couldn't say to her still that she was better off. You couldn't tell her what was clear and evident. You come to a certain point and it's too much a cost. You have to be able to recognize that. You couldn't just say good riddance, maybe. You couldn't just be heartless. But you have to recognize.

"Is there something you need?" he asks. "Anything?"

There comes a muffled, fumbling sound, a breath of static, maybe her voice beginning to mumble something. He's not certain what he hears.

"What was it you said before?" he asks, just at the sound of the hang-up, speaking on through into the drone of the dial tone. "She'll want to know."

---

Neither Dwight nor Russell can seem to find a place to sit in Helen's house. Their grandmother, in the old house, had always kept a single room to be in company order—the furniture all arranged in such a way, the breakables all placed exactly, and nothing ever touched but to be cleaned and dusted. Under no circumstances were the children to enter in. She'd kept a string tied across the doorway to mind them off.

Helen's whole house seems like that. The main room could be most of the space of Dwight and Trina's whole house. It's furnished like a showroom, of course. A statuette of a greyhound dog sits at either foot of the staircase that winds up to the second floor landing and around and down again. There are framed paintings of race-horses and sailboats and of flowers in vases. Two big brass urns sit on either side of the entryway door, each with some tall treelike plant growing out of it, the leaves like palm fronds.

The one big couch is white leather. There's a big lounge chair, the seat covered in throw cushions in careful placement. There's a divan that Trina and Helen occupy together. They neither one look comfortably seated; it's such an odd-shaped thing, made so that a person has to half-lay and half-sit.

Helen has said for Dwight and Russell to make themselves to home, urged them to. Dwight feels for her distress, though not enough to seat himself on white leather. "I'm better standing," Dwight says, "my back." Russell only shrugs. He has begun to drift back toward the entryway.

Trina glares at Dwight. She's justified, he knows. It's ill behavior not wanting to accept Helen's welcome. It's childishness. He sees it in himself and is not willing to get around it.

"Company!" John James's voice enters in ahead of him. There's the sound of the heavy entryway door being let slam and of his quick footsteps clapping across the wood floor. "Hello! How's everybody?" He catches Russell's hand going by and slaps him on the shoulder, and Russell is pulled back some ways into the main room. He grabs Dwight's arm around the biceps and squeezes, saying, "Hello, brute." It's the same way he goes about electioneering—patting backs, handshaking. It's the same put-on. Friend to everybody. Nonetheless, Dwight is relieved for his finally being there.

His own greeting is overfriendly and loud. Russell too is made uncommonly enthused. For a brief while the three men carry on amongst each other as if unknowing of the women's presence. That stops abruptly.

"Don't everybody start spitting," Trina says, her tone enough a mix of joking and ire to call them back around without causing too much an upset. Russell moves off at once, claiming a space of wall to lean against and cross his arms.

Dwight feels the awkwardness of being in Helen's house come upon him again. He looks for his brother-in-law to recommence his offhand talk, but John James as well seems tensed up and doubtful now.

"Helen?" John James says. He trails off, rubbing the palms of his hands together, grimacing as if suffering some twinge of something.

Helen hunches her shoulders up a little but doesn't move or respond otherwise.

John James drops his hands to his sides and begins a swinging motion. After a moment he stills that, wipes his hands on his pant legs, and slips them into his pockets. The sound of coins and keys being jingled together interrupts the worried quiet for a while. He stops that when it seems to come to him what noise he's making. He rests his hands on his hips then, the look on his face like he's trying to bring some difficult matter of work or politics to resolution in his mind and is not able to.

"Somebody name it then," Helen says. "Go ahead."

"Let's just us visit awhile," Trina says. "There's nothing that's that important."

"Well, it's what we're here for," Helen says.

"It's not all what we're here for," Trina says. "We're here to visit. We can visit awhile."

Helen smiles at Trina and puts out her hand for Trina to take and squeeze in both of hers.

"Let's just get it said and done," Helen says. She looks in the direction of Dwight, John James, and Russell, not settling her gaze on any single one of them. "Somebody," she says.

Dwight has stood on his feet to the point where his back feels compressed on him. He has to move around now, one hip stuck out in avoidance of the pressing ache. "Timber prices are up right now," he says, "way up."

He looks to catch the other men's expressions. Russell is blanked out behind his sun shades, keeping hidden, keeping as far out of the danger zone as he can manage. John James nods his head as Dwight speaks. It's just the posture of his body that shows distractedness now. He has moved to sit on the arm of the couch. His hands are on his knees. He is rocking slightly. Tight as a bowstring, Dwight thinks. That's exactly the expression that fits.

"I understand twenty-three for pine," Dwight says. "Poplar would be more. Maple and oak more, of course. I believe we'd want to lease thirty acres at least." He shrugs the way he's practiced in his mind doing. "Forty acres. That's to be decided on when we get the buyer's appraisal though."

Helen doesn't look at him, or anybody, directly just then. She has her hair done with reddish streaks this week. Her makeup—eyeshade, lipstick, whatever—looks to have been applied more to hide than add to. It fades her complexion more than improving it. What look of health she'd shown the past few weeks is lost and gone now. After a moment she sighs like she is considering what to say. John James clears his throat, but does not change his position any.

They're not looking at one another, Dwight realizes, Helen is not looking at John James and John James is not looking at Helen. He keeps on talking a few minutes. He's not being listened to by anybody, he knows, but he dreads to stop now. He dreads to stop speaking and have nobody else start.

"I'm determined to go visit the place," Helen says then. "Can't we at least go and look around."

"That all right with everybody?" John James says, looking at Dwight for his answer. "We all go over there and look around? Not make no definite plans this minute?"

"That's fine," Dwight says.

It's when they are driving home that evening that Trina tells them. "She miscarried again," she says.

Dwight glances into the rearview mirror before responding. He finds Russell staring back, his shades off now. The skin around Russell's eyes is paler-looking than the rest of his face. The whites are clear of any redness, Dwight believes. The pupils don't look abnormal in any way.

"Miscarried," Dwight says. He pauses, then adds, "again."

"Miscarried," Trina says, "again."

It seems a far longer time than it actually is before anybody in the car speaks once more.

---

It's even wilder-looking here than Dwight remembers. The old house is still in the clear mostly, though the front yard is thick with milkweed and thistle. Heavier brush has rooted on the slope as far up as the well box—patches of saw briars, a few laurel bushes. The barn lot is inside the tree line now. An oak, sprouted from the mast of the old hog pen, heaves against the barn's eastward corner, pushing logs askew by the force of its growth. The barn is halfway fallen-in and so overgrown it's untelling where the brush ends and the building begins. Creeper vines wind between logs, through door and window gaps, from ground level upwards to the loft and across the slanted roof, taking the structure as by a knowing will.

Dwight steps out of the truck, studying the ground a moment before he sets his foot down. He wades a few paces toward the house through weeds up to his knees. "You-all watch where you step," he says. He glances over his shoulder at the rest of the clan.

Trina is carrying Dreama on her hip, though the child is making motions to be let loose. As frail, as puny-looking as she is, Dreama gives her mother no easy time. Trina puts her on the ground but keeps hold of her hand. Dreama resists against even this, running in place against her mother's grasp, leaning her body in the direction she wants to dash off in.

"Let's none of us get snake-bit," Dwight yells. He walks toward the well box, a square formation of mortared-together stone that stands just higher than the seed stalks of the grass. He climbs upon it, the back of his neck tingling at his own mind's suggestion of a coiled-up copperhead.

He watches Helen and John James walk around toward the house. They keep an arm's-length distance. They are not speaking that Dwight can tell, though their heads are inclined in such a way as to be mindful of one another. Once or twice John James reaches his hand as if to steady Helen, though she has not stumbled or shown much sign at all of what weakness she must feel, what distress. Each time his hand moves toward her, she steps the least bit further away.

*Miscarried.* It sounds like a word to name some bad act somebody has done. Or had done to them. The way Helen looks, it's not like she's upset only, not like she's just depressed. She is ashamed-looking. It's just a bad-sounding word, is all.

He cannot see where Russell has gone to. Dreama has lined toward the barn lot though, her mother right after her. The child has some purpose in mind, Dwight knows. She's seen something, or thought she's seen something, that she has to get hold of or die. Dwight doesn't follow yet. From where he stands he can make out more of the contours of the place, the ground's unevenness seeable even beneath the brush cover.

His memory of the place is not as strong as Helen's. He hadn't been much older than Dreama when their mamaw and papaw both had died. In his mind he has them both dying at the same time. He can recall details of only a single funeral, a single burial. He knows they had died almost a year apart. The story told is that their papaw died out somewhere on the place, out somewhere working, of a heart attack or a stroke; what he knows of their mamaw is that she hadn't died at home but in the regional hospital at Hazard.

The shape of the stone fence between the yard and road can be recognized still. In among the wildness overgrowing it are trumpet vines and purple phlox, patches of sweet william, a few daylilies. He cannot remember the place the way it probably had been, weeds cut back to the tree edges, mowed grass. He does suddenly recall two car tires that had been set out in the yard as flower planters. They were painted white. The old people all had had those.

Dreama and her mother have wandered out of sight now and probably far enough away to be worried about. Dwight steps away from the well box and angles toward the path they have left in the grass. We'll have to look one another over for ticks, he thinks. A crawling sensation comes over his scalp and neck, and he takes off his cap to search his fingers through his hair, feeling for anything dug in or moving.

He finds them up toward the house with Helen and John James. Dwight feels shy coming upon them. Whatever conversation it is they're having, Helen and John James and Trina, they let come to an end at Dwight's approach. He wishes they had not seen him coming so that he could have slipped around the barn and on down toward the old pasture.

What he does instead is grab Dreama up in a hug and turn her upside down, a trick that makes the child laugh out of control for a while. She feels oddly more heavy to him than he knows she should. He is able to set her on her feet again without hurting himself, though he has been made shakily uncertain of his strength.

He is relieved for the chance to stand and rest for a minute and stare with the others at the old house. The porch roof has completely fallen in on the front side and is about to all the way around, the corner pillars each shoved askew, the banister rail and slats broken almost to kindling. The windows all are out and one of the chimneys has begun to lose stones; the other stands complete still but leans so sharply it seems more likely to tumble over than to keep standing. Dwight hopes that Helen will be content to keep to the outside. He'd not want to go inside the old place and have it decide to collapse on them.

"It's a shame," Trina says. "Ain't they no way it could be repaired?"

“Maybe if you tear it down to the foundation,” Dwight says. “Tear it down and build it over again.”

“It’s a shame,” Trina says.

Dwight has not told her about Shondra calling. He believes it was her. It must have been. He didn’t dream it. It was her. She should have told him where she was. That’s all she would have had to say. Where she was. He’d have gone and got her. Sore back, middle of the night, it wouldn’t have mattered. She had just to say the word. He would have gone. Wherever she was. Whatever shape she was in. He would have gone and got her and brought her to the house.

He feels a tug on his arm, Dreama wanting to be let loose. He hadn’t been completely aware that he was still holding on to her. He doesn’t let go of her right away still. He realizes Trina is watching him. “Let’s walk on around this way,” he says. He waits for Trina to decide to come before he lets Dreama loose.

They trail Dreama back down the slope of the yard. The little girl looks at them over her shoulder as she goes, hurrying, determined not to be caught up with. Dwight does not call after her, though it is all his will not to. They lose sight of her as she passes beyond the barn. Dwight does not hurry yet. He is already feeling a little bit of a tenderness down low in his spine. The last thing he wants is to be sprawled on the ground in front of everybody, to have to be helped back to the truck by John James and Russell.

Old boards, black with rot, are stacked against the long side of the barn—all different lengths and thicknesses. There’s a sheet of corrugated tin, a roll of chicken wire grown through with horseweeds, some piles of burlap sacks. “I’d hate to think what-all’s been left laying around this place,” Dwight says.

“Might be a treasure of old money,” Trina says.

Dwight laughs. “No,” he says.

They sight Dreama again as soon as they pass the corner of the barn. She is standing a dozen yards further, in high grass, staring down at her feet. Dwight is not sure what to make of her pose, of the expression on her face, like she is hypnotized. He shouts at the instant the image comes to his mind, "Snake!" And then he is hurrying, pain warnings or not.

It's just a moment of time that the whole event occurs in, not half a minute. Dwight has gotten no more than a step or two before Dreama begins kneeling down, begins reaching her hand into the grass. He shouts again, "Dreama!" But the child shows no sign of heeding him, even of hearing him.

Russell appears then, stepping over a fallen rail of what's left of the pasture fence, his loose shirttail catching in whatever brush or briars he's passing through.

Dwight has had an idea about Russell that he's not told his brother yet, that he's barely let himself indulge in yet, which is Russell coming to work with him when he buys his truck. He's not been sure enough to mention it. It's wishful thinking to believe Russell is turned around enough to be relied on. Dwight wonders if he is high right now, if maybe he slipped off to burn one.

Russell is saying something to Dreama. The girl has her head turned to him, speaking back. He is not rushing to her. They are talking, is all, and he is just strolling toward her, like haste is no matter. But he is kneeling beside her before Dwight or Trina are even half the distance they need to make. He looks up at them as they hurry forward.

"It's a terrapin," he says.

"A terrapin?" Trina says. "Lord, my heart's going a mile a minute. I thought sure it was a snake. Dwight, you said it was a snake."

It might well have been a snake, Dwight thinks. He doesn't say it though. His own heart feels like it's about to burst inside him, it's pumping so hard. He feels dizzy a little bit. Just because this time it wasn't, he thinks. Just because this time it wasn't don't mean next time it won't be.

Helen's voice comes from nearby then. "What is it?" she shouts. She and John James have already come past the barn. They are not running, though they must have been. They are walking fast, John James holding Helen's elbow.

"It's nothing," Trina calls back. "It's all right."

Dreama is poking at the terrapin with a grass stem. The creature is pulled only partway into its shell. Its legs still are out, its mouth is showing, its eyes can be seen. They all keep quiet, the whole family, watching as Dreama motions the grass stem about the terrapin's head, about its black eyes, about its half-open mouth. The terrapin's shell is a faintly checkered pattern of yellow and black. It could be a clump of dead leaves, a patch of shadowy ground. They would not see it if they were not standing so close upon it. They might not see it again if they looked away.

It's not until Dreama picks up the terrapin to hold in her lap that they seem to realize one another's presence again and all step a little bit apart from one another. Where they stand is the little flat of land that must have been the garden plot. A few hard furrows can yet be felt by stamping amongst the weeds. The garden's boundaries can no longer be seen, though on the hill slopes on either side the terraces, the places where extra patches of corn were grown, can be made out still.

What remains of the orchard are just a few scattered trees, scrubby and wild-looking, the branches showing only scant fruit and it blighted and knotty. The orchard and garden plot both are so wholly entangled in brush and briar as to have never before been tended. "Why, it'd take a man six months to clear all this out," Dwight says.

"I don't reckon we're planning to, are we?" Helen asks.

Dwight looks to the ridgeline east of them. In view are red and white oaks, yellow poplar, and no end of pine, a few decent-sized black walnut scattered about. He envisions a line from there northward and then back around to the south, indicating the boundaries of the timber to be cut. Thirty acres, at least, he thinks, forty acres, to be profitable. Sixty.

He can feel Helen looking at him, waiting for him to speak. He can feel them all waiting for him to speak. He kicks at the ground for a moment, then kneels down despite the warning twinge in his back.

He begins to dig into the dirt with his fingers. In a short while he comes up with some dirt-clotted object, an old hoe blade or ax head, some manner of old lost tool. "Why, what purpose would they be in it?" he replies.